THE MARGARET-GHOST

Also by Barbara Novak

NOVELS
Alice's Neck

NON-FICTION
American Painting of the Nineteenth Century
Nature and Culture

PLAYS
The Ape and the Whale

THE
Margaret-Ghost

a novel by

BARBARA NOVAK

GEORGE BRAZILLER, PUBLISHER

New York

First published in 2003 by George Braziller, Inc.

For information, please contact the publisher:
George Braziller, Inc.
171 Madison Avenue
New York, NY 10016

Library of Congress Cataloging-in-Publication Data:

Novak, Barbara.
    The Margaret-ghost : a novel / by Barbara Novak.
        p.   cm.
    ISBN 0-8076-1524-2
    1. Fuller, Margaret, 1810-1850—Fiction. 2. Biography as a literary form—Fiction. 3. Women authors—Fiction. 4. Biographers—Fiction. 5. Feminists—Fiction. I. Title.

PS3564.O886M37 2003
813'.54—dc21   2003050339

Printed and bound in the United States of America
Designed by Rita Lascaro

For Brian O'Doherty

ACKNOWLEDGMENTS

This book could not have been written without the work of the meticulous scholars who produced Angelica Bookbinder's reading list. I am especially thankful for the pioneering gathering of primary materials by Bell Gale Chevigny that first aroused my interest in Margaret Fuller, and for the scrupulous editions of Fuller's letters by Robert N. Hudspeth that brought her mind and thoughts so vividly to life. George Braziller's immediate enthusiasm warmed my heart. Julia Klein's fresh alertness to every detail made working with her a joy. Vicki Rosenberg's solicitude has been invaluable. I am deeply grateful to my friend, Victoria Newhouse, for her steady encouragement. Maia Gregory, Patrick Merla and the Novak family were early supporters of *The Margaret-Ghost*, as was my husband, Brian O'Doherty, who has given me the intellectual companionship and love that Margaret always sought.

Yes, it is only love, that heaven on earth, that can make any mortal cease for a moment to be lonely.

— MARGARET FULLER

It is not woman, but the law of right, the law of growth, that speaks in us, and demands the perfection of each being in its kind—apple as apple, woman as woman.

— MARGARET FULLER

The unquestionably haunting Margaret-ghost . . . What comes up is the wonderment of *why* she may . . . be felt as haunting . . . this singular woman who would, though conceit was imputed to her, doubtless have been surprised to know that talk may be still, after more than half a century, made about her . . . the Margaret-ghost, as I have ventured to call it, still unmistakably walks the old passages.

— HENRY JAMES, 1903

1

There is no grave to visit. At Père-Lachaise, Proust is buried with his family under a black marble slab. Wilde's monument has a penis broken by vandals, who inscribe messages of love and hate all over Epstein's stone sculpture. Sarah Bernhardt's grave, not far from Molière and La Fontaine, is perversely hidden from visitors who circle mindlessly, grave maps in hand asking: Where is she? Where?

But Margaret's body was never found. I've always loved to visit the graves of the great—of those I know only through their earthly accomplishments: a cherished book, a memorable poem, a great painting, an historic act, a life of political achievement—because for me they are pedestalled but distanced heroes. I don't feel the same pain of loss I would feel for family or friends who have shared my days. Often, I hardly know what they looked like. They are simply dear friends of spirit, sufficiently defleshed from my own blood and tears that I can love them in that special angle in my heart reserved for the singular men and women who comprise our history and culture. I don't count myself their equal. So I don't cry over them. Yet their graves exert a curious fascination, cosseting, as it were, their mortal remains.

But Margaret never left a grave. In that loss I discover a different kind of pain, one exacerbated by her absent bones. I can only pay homage to her by a trip to Fire Island, where I stand on the shore by the illimitable sea. That sea that Margaret always dreaded. That sea that swallowed her up as she returned to America from Italy. That swallowed her child and her (possible) husband, the Marchese d'Ossoli.

It was from his coat that Thoreau, walking on the strand, ripped the button. Held it up to the light. Pondered mortality: "An *actual* button so called—and yet all the life it is connected with is less substantial to me than my faintest dreams . . . We are ever dying to one world and being born into another, and possibly no man knows whether he is at any time dead in the sense in which he affirms that phenomenon of another, or not."

A monument to them all at Mount Auburn, finally erected by the Fuller family, houses the remains of the child, dug up from the dunes not long after he perished. But Margaret is not there (though one unconfirmed rumor has her buried in an unmarked grave in Coney Island). Her bones do not inhabit that dust. Her ghost may not be there either. Yet it haunts me.

I cannot escape the Margaret-Ghost. My future depends on it. I have set myself to writing a study of one of the most intriguing women of the nineteenth century, author of *Woman in the Nineteenth Century*, friend of Thoreau and Emerson, of Mazzini and Mickiewicz, of Horace Greeley and George Sand. I take on the task in the midst of the feminist wars of the 1990s, when anything I say or write about woman, gender, sexuality, is subject to criticism and dissent. Can the simple fact of my own womanness sustain me? Is there enough commonality to carry me through? Because I need the book to continue my life, my career. My academic tenure depends on it. The English department of my college (small, distinguished, situated in Boston) has given me a year's leave from teaching to research Margaret's papers at the Houghton Library in Cambridge. From my apartment in Boston, on the corner of Dartmouth and Newbury Streets, I can look out at the Boston Public Library and see in my mind's eye the Puvis de Chavannes murals inside, and then also walk along Boston Common to the Greek wine bar on West Street that once housed the offices of *The Dial*, where Margaret, supervised by Emerson's critical eye, edited the transcendental tracts and where she held the famous "Conversations" to shape women who would "understand and share" her goals.

The department wants the book as soon as possible. My time is running out. I've already done a good bit of the research, but the contradictions of history are drowning me as Margaret drowned in the sea. Who or what am I to believe?

What is my role as biographer? As historian? Which known facts should I choose? Which are irrefutable, absolute?

Not her marriage—even her alleged husband's sister didn't know of it until after the child was born. Not her death—whether reaching for a plank to brave the waves or clinging to the forecastle with her husband and the child she refused to abandon until a wave washed her away. And *all the time, all the time,* the reports indicate, the scavengers watched from the nearby shore, and, over a period of about 12 hours, while the boat was cracking up, could have saved them all, except they didn't know anyone aboard was worth saving. As if any life, any human life would not have been reason enough.

But it was MARGARET they didn't save, and somehow it breaks my heart. As she always told everyone, she had so much to offer. Immodest, but true.

Which unknown facts will always elude me? If I knew more, would my portrait of her be substantially different? And then there is the matter of self-revelation. I am the author, the biographer. The chooser of facts. The screener of History, which has already contributed its own measure of attrition, of deletion of time, of moments she lived. Yet her moments and mine must coalesce in some way, if I'm to penetrate her life.

Both women. At least that in common, although Joel Myerson and Robert Hudspeth have done meticulous work on her. Writers. That, too. I dream sometimes of seeing my name on the cover:

MARGARET FULLER

(or better)

THE MARGARET-GHOST

By Angelica Bookbinder

Both thinkers. Ah. I can't pretend to come near her. Incomparably erudite. By the age of eight, she had read the *Aeneid* in the original. Even Emerson was intimidated by her.

Really? you ask. Not possible.

Really. Melville called him a Plato who talked through his nose. Margaret also called him a Plato, or "Greek," but she could hold her own with him. They were so intense in each other's presence, they often communicated in the same house through notes and messages. Making Lidian (Mrs. Emerson, who, after all, had changed her name from Lydia to please the Great Man for whom she competed with his dead wife Ellen, whose coffin he had opened after her death—a slightly different kind of grave visiting, we might say) cry with envy.

There was only one Margaret, as Poe acknowledged. But even her name had changed. She was born with the preface of Sarah: "I do not like Sarah. Call me Margaret alone, pray do!" I can only write of her as Woman, using the capital with which her gender was so often denoted. As a full woman—how else?

To write of her only as an intellectual, as a philosophical model, as a feminist even, would leave out too much. Too much of what was, ultimately, important about her. But she evades ordinary biography. She requires more invention than that. So though I am aware that my much desired tenure, my future scholarly reputation, might depend on the exactness of what I will tell of her, I will have to leave it to others to decide on the viability of my portrayal. I see her, after all, through the screen of more than 140 intervening years. Through History, not always accommodating. Through her words, which still carry traces of her long-past emotion. Through her loves (so often unrequited). And through her tragedies, which were ultimately more than she deserved (though her death was considered suitably romantic by some.)

How hazardous to try to organize the chaos of life onto the printed page. To transmit life to print is impossible. Yet language, with all its limitations, is one of our few facilitators. How to reconstruct a life, A LIFE, out of Margaret's own words, letters, journals, articles, books, dispatches from the war in Italy? Which of the contemporary accounts of her to credit? Hawthorne, who is alleged to have loathed her? Emerson, who surely loved her some? The women she loved, or the men? What was love to her? Or marriage? What was it to be Woman?

For all that she wrote, all she declaimed, it is still hard to discern her true feelings. She ran too deep. She was too complex. There were, in effect, too many Margarets, yet each perhaps true to a part of her. What has she left behind her? Endless words. Texts on a page. Testimonials to her manner of written discourse, her eloquence, her poetry, her literary voice. But there were no films then, to record her body language, the palpability of her body. To observe her brain working—that remarkable brain. To capture her walk, the sound of her voice.

I need to hear that voice. The sounds as they escape the throat. Rumor has it that they were nasal. (Poe, however, thought them musical.) What were the intonations, the pauses, the rhythms? Poe says she spoke deliberately, drawing her words out "as long as possible." How did she move when she spoke? One contemporary observer noticed that she tended to look at her shoulders, as though admiring them. What of the eyes that observed the shoulders? Did the shortsighted eyes always blink as disconcertingly as Emerson claimed when he first met her? Did the well-endowed bosom heave? Her person, her physical person, is missing. How do I flesh out the Margaret-Ghost? What special elixir can bring her to life?

Some of the details are in my files; the files are multicolored. The expensive laminated folders sold today in stationery shops: PURPLE. RED. BLUE. YELLOW. BLACK. To keep the job, the task, from drying out, becoming boring (as if it were possible for Margaret ever to bore), I avoid the standard buff manila folders.

Now I spread a rainbow fan of them on the long table before me. It is putting together the puzzle that baffles me. This is, even more than some, a difficult life to grasp. Margaret has left too many clues. Then again, not enough. I have to begin somewhere. I reach for the blue. The P's are in the blue folder: Physical. Phrenological. Psychological. Personal horoscope. My categories, as you can see from the last, are sometimes logical only to me. Yet how can a horoscope be anything but personal? It stays with the P's.

2

A. *The Physical Margaret*

Two bits of evidence: an anonymous 1846 daguerreotype and an 1848 painting by Thomas Hicks.

Margaret, to judge from the daguerreotype, was not photogenic. Perhaps I'm put off by the hairstyle, modish at the time, but, I feel, most unbecoming: hair parted in the center, two forward portions looped into braids that circle each ear, rather like picture frames, linked to a braided coronet at the crown. The sectioning of the hair—first centrally, then across the crown—is tightly pulled and reveals too much scalp, almost as if those portions have been shaved. Her mouth, presumably turned down in thought over the book she reads, seems more sour than meditative; her eyes, downcast, bulge under the lids, as if caught in one of her famously repetitious blinks. Her nose is too large and a bit lumpy.

I cannot see from this photographic simulacrum the feature later remarked upon by Oliver Wendell Holmes who went to school with her as a child: "her long and flexible neck, arching and undulating—strange undulating movements which one who loved her would compare to a swan, and those who loved her not to the ophidian who tempted our common mother." Poor Margaret, so often compared to swan or serpent. Yet in neither guise does she seem a temptress. On the whole, she does not seem attractive. In fact, she offers justification to those who called her plain, though after her death, when Emerson called her that, her mother cried.

But photography, in 1846, was still in its infancy. Not yet adept perhaps at capturing the soul, at floating the spirit up to the surface to transform and transfuse the plain features. The Indians surely thought this possible. Some refused to pose for the camera. It would steal the spirit. The spirit would be gone forever. Though if they thought about the sacred bones so highly prized after death, surely those would not contain the spirit, either. The spirit would have gone to the Happy Hunting Ground, as even Margaret's friend Thoreau suggested. And Margaret was most sympathetic to the Indians, after all, outraged at the tragic aspect of an Indian who had been dislodged from his village, which still housed the bones of his ancestors, to make way for white settlers: "What feelings must consume their hearts at such moments! I scarcely see how they can forbear to shoot the white man where he stands." Margaret, bless her, cared about the disenfranchised.

Do I deceive myself in claiming that the daguerreotype was simply not a great photograph? A great photographer, a Lewis Carroll perhaps, might have known better how to handle the mechanical device, might have been able to capture the soul through the new technology. ANONYMOUS, operating out of the popular Plumb's gallery in New York, was not a great photographer.

She is better served by the painter Thomas Hicks, who two years later, in Italy, rejected her love (a not uncommon experience for her) but painted her with a floating brush that somehow transmitted a touch of spirit. Margaret reflective, reddish brown hair (referred to as light by many who knew her, including Emerson and Poe) fortunately pulled back—but not braided—perhaps held (we cannot see it) by the blue chenille cord she often used for that task, face harshly planar now, but no longer as plain, nose nicely chiselled (*lumps lost*), features finer, like those of her (prettier) mother and sister. A hint of family attractiveness—aura through association. The lumps remain, however, in the sagging bosom, but something staid is relieved by the purplish blue sheen of the dress. By the soft fringe of her light shawl. Do the gondolas in the distance enhance the romantic air, or is it the flow of the painter's brush? Perhaps the fact that the statue behind her is an Eros. But which of them, painter or sitter, dictated the Eros connection?

A need for love, intimacy, had dominated all her close relationships. She thirsted for it, railed against those she loved for their lack of equal sentiment, if not their rejection.

When she maintained that it was "so true that a woman may be in love with a woman and a man with a man," what did woman's love of woman mean to her? Could it remain *agape*, or did it slide, even if not sexually acted upon, into Eros? Emerson claimed that her friendships "as a girl with girls, as a woman with women, were not unmingled with passion, and had passages of romantic sacrifice and of ecstatic fusion, which I have heard with the ear, but could not trust my profane pen to report."

I will not deal here with Emerson's profane pen. His piety always prevailed over his profanity. But he raises the issue of Margaret's passion. Margaret and Love. A genuine problem. For all my enlightened concepts of woman's professional role, I have not been aware of having erotic feelings for another woman. Yet am I absolutely certain I never had them? Surely I understand friendship, love of woman friends, sisterhood. If I try to probe my feelings honestly, would, could it be enough?

As to my relations with men, so far they are only a bit better than Margaret's. An early marriage, long over, entered into more with curiosity than feeling. Several liaisons with Harvard intellectuals, generally initiated with eyes too wide open for sentiment, and always subordinate to the academic demands of graduate school, dissertation, and finally the mad busyness of the young raw academic at the bottom of the ladder. Nothing like the agonies of the unrequited Margaret seems to have undergone.

But back to the painting. Did she choose to be seated here, near the Gothic arcade of the Doge's Palace, with a

courting couple behind her, looking out at the Grand
Venetian Canal? Did she want to remind the artist of her
love for him as he probed her features for her spirit? Earlier
she had written to him:

                                          Rome 23 April 1847
Dear Youth,
       You do not come to see me ... I do not understand
     why you do not seek me more ... I want to know and to
     love you and to have you love me ... How can you let me
     pass you by, without full and free communication ... Very
     soon I must go from here, do not let me go without giving
     me some of your life. I wish this for both our sakes, for
     mine, because I have so lately been severed from congen-
     ial companionship, that I am suffering for want of it, for
     yours, because I feel as if I had something precious to leave
     in your charge.

Something precious to leave in your charge. She always felt
that those she loved did not recognize what she had to give.
She acknowledged, insisted upon, even, her own precious
value. The rebuke was always there.

       By the time the painting was completed, she had perhaps
already married Ossoli, or not married him, since the evidence is so contradictory. But Hicks, who after her death
spoke of her in brotherly terms, had still been placed in the
awkward position of rejecting her. In doing so, he claimed
that his heart had grown gray. But Margaret always *demanded*
love. Two years before her death, in the same year that he
painted her, she wrote him a letter containing her last wishes.

Rome 17 May 1848
You would say to those I leave behind that I was willing to
die . . . I have wished to be natural and true, but the world
was not in harmony with me—nothing came right for me.

She had not been well. She had money problems. Her
good friends Mickiewicz and Mazzini were already in Italy,
where the political situation had worsened. She was living
on the Corso, where the people were restless and angry at
the Pope, and the Civic Guard, in which Ossoli served, had a
few weeks earlier occupied the city gates.

She was already pregnant when she posed for the painting. With Ossoli's child, who was born in September. She
was pregnant when she left the artist her farewell letter in
case of death. A year later still, in October 1849, she wrote to
Samuel Gray Ward (who said after her death, "How can you
describe a Force? How can you write the life of Margaret?")
that she had "loved [Hicks] very much; we have been very
intimate."

Intimate? What was intimacy for her? If we accept that
it is now a euphemism for sexual relations, surely in the
nineteenth century, in Margaret's hands, it meant something
else. Yet we know she had also been "intimate" with Ossoli,
since she bore the child who shocked her New England
friends, creating the mystery of the marriage/non-marriage
that has tantalized History. Had the New England virgin
finally succumbed to the advice of the European sophisticate
Mickiewicz when he warned her she would not be a full
woman until she relinquished her virgin state? An enthusi-

astic Margaret admired Sand and De Staël and even the
shocking French actress Rachel. Once on European soil, did
she develop a different sense of virtue and morality?

Why would the great intellectual New England Brahmin
marry an untutored Italian who could not even read her
erudite treatises were they written in his own language? In
the same letter to Ward, she wrote, "Ossoli is a good companion to me here. . . ." To someone else a month later, "My
relation to Ossoli has been like retiring to one of those gentle lovely places in the woods—something of the violet has
been breathed into my life, and will never pass away."

The woman Hicks painted loved him how? What did he
float to the surface that the camera could not grasp? She was
capable of so many loves. She offered herself, yes offered, on
myriad levels. To Emerson, to Ward, to Hicks, to James
Nathan, the ultimate betrayer, who refused to return her letters and then PUBLISHED them! And after all that. She gave
herself. To Ossoli. Physically and emotionally. To Ossoli who
by her own admission knew "nothing of books."

This bookish Margaret-Ghost. This extraordinary intellectual. This formidable feminist, who had also offered love to
Caroline Sturgis, to Anna Barker, and, perhaps—who
knows?—to other women still unrevealed and unknown.

B. *The Phrenological*

She had her bumps analyzed. In November 1837, when the
twenty-seven-year-old Margaret was teaching at the Greene
Street School in Providence, Rhode Island, Orson Squire

Fowler, who never travelled without his measuring tape, took Margaret's head into his hands and allowed his fingers to analyze her bumps. Literally, she had, as they say, her head examined. Fowler, as part of a publishing family, was later to publish Margaret's writings and crusade for such women's rights as freedom from tightly laced corsets—a cause that gained Margaret's full approval. Perhaps that is why, in addition to her probable pregnancy, she seemed lumpy in Hicks' painting. But Fowler, examining her "bumps," seemed disinterested at that earlier moment in "lumps." Rather, his fingers, called "sentient" by an observer, traced out in the configurations of her skull the faculty of "excessive IDEALITY." Almost 50 years after her death, the *Phrenological Journal* was still discussing Margaret's Ideality.

According to *Fowler's Practical Phrenology*, which he published in 1846, four years before Margaret's death and only nine after he had examined her head, ideality could be located on Fowler's chart as part of Species III, Semi-Intellectual Sentiments, mixed faculties partaking of both human sentiment and intellect: "THEY ARE LOCATED PARTLY BETWEEN THE FOREHEAD AND THE PORTIONS OF THE HEAD COVERED BY HAIR, AND PARTLY WITHIN THE LATTER, GIVING, WHEN LARGE OR VERY LARGE, A FULLNESS AND BREADTH TO THIS PORTION OF THE HEAD. . . ."

So Margaret's excessive ideality predisposed her to love poetry, fiction, and what was then called "truth" and "beauty." If it was as large as indicated, presumably it measured 167 on Fowler's scale of phrenological organs. All this is quite obvious from the Hicks portrait, which in its semi-frontal stance gives us a highly clarified view of Margaret's "ideal" forehead (called capacious by Poe, who did not always admire her). Unfortunately, we cannot also read from this pose what the back of Margaret's head was like. (Rumor had it that after their deaths Ossoli's skull had been retrieved, but this remains in the arena of speculation.) We do not, in any case, have the skull that Fowler's fingers so sentiently probed. We do not, therefore, have any means of judging from this portrait one of Fowler's most interesting categories: the various manifestations of AMATIVENESS, specifically Fuller's amativeness, located at the back of the head.

We do, however, have a clue in the phrenological report of yet another practitioner, the journalist John Neal, who examined Margaret's bumps after Fowler, and was reported by Sarah Helen Whitman (a poet who became Poe's Helen) to have found that her amativeness struggled with her ADHESIVENESS.

Another Whitman, the illustrious Walt, placed great stress on adhesiveness, which in nineteenth-century parlance referred sometimes to same-sex friendship and sometimes to same-sex love. He admitted the latter proclivity to Oscar Wilde, who shared his penchant. But Whitman also claimed to have fathered six children, a feat never proven. Margaret had only the one child, but feasibly her adhesiveness echoed Walt's. She loved women as well as men. Perhaps even better. Perhaps, too, I am dealing here not so much with bisexuality as with love—love with all of its concomitant problematics.

C. *The Psychological*

If, lacking the back of her skull, we can tell little phrenologically about Margaret's amativeness, can more recent psychological developments, i.e., the lessons of Sigmund Freud, instruct us as to the known objects of her amativeness? To the earliest objects, her parents? Here I hesitate. This is not meant to be a psycho-biography. But all earlier writers have placed great stress on the education *inflicted* upon her by her father. She herself regretted it. But she would not have been MARGARET without it.

TIMOTHY FULLER: Harvard-trained lawyer and two-term congressman who ultimately became Speaker of the Massachusetts House. Determined to educate Margaret, his first-born, as he would a son, he instructed her in Latin and English grammar at age six, inculcating in her the heroic ideals of action of the ancient Romans, causing her to have blood nightmares after reading Virgil, making her a "victim of spectral illusions, nightmares and somnambulism," giving her headaches and migraines for the rest of her life. It has been suggested that Margaret developed resultantly a feminine Oedipus or Electra Complex.

Cf. Freud, *The Ego and the Id:*
Analysis very often shows that a little girl, after she has had to relinquish her father as a love object, will bring her masculinity into prominence and identify herself with her father (that is, with the object which has been lost) instead of her mother. This will clearly depend on whether the masculinity in her disposition—whatever that might consist in—is strong enough.

Margaret did indeed dream frequently of her mother's death.

MARGARETT CRANE FULLER: Associated by Margaret
with the Garden. Of a "fair and flower-like" nature. Her
mother's secluded garden, a favorite meditative place for
young Margaret, was "full of choice flowers and fruit-
trees." In nineteenth-century floral language, flowers were
complex symbols of the affections: the tulip, according to
one flower dictionary, was the symbol of violent love; the
linden tree of conjugal love; the blue canterbury-bell of
constancy. The same dictionary speaks of *coldness: to live
without love*, symbolized by the Agnus Castus, an autumnal
shrub with whorled spikes of blue and white flowers. Pliny
wrote of the priestesses of Ceres who formed their virginal
couches of branches of Agnus Castus. A poem below the
floral description notes that,
      "The frigid and unfeeling thrive the best / And a warm
heart in this cold world is like / a beacon light, wasting its
feeble frame / Upon the wintry deep, that feels it not, /
And trembling, with each pitiless gust, that blows / till its
faint fire is spent."

Was the Agnus Castus Margaret's floral curse? To live in
the cold, without love? Was it that desperation that caused
her always to castigate the reluctant targets of her affection
for withholding from her what she needed? What special
symbolism had the Garden (including the Biblical Garden
enclosed) and the flower for Margaret? She claimed that her
mother's garden stood, in her mind, "as the emblem of
domestic love." Yet domestic love was not the same to her as
the perfect and ideal love she sought. Her mother's garden,
though, was "a nest" in which her "thoughts could lie fallow

and be fed and kept warm." Did she think of her thought as organic? As flowering? The Roman moralists whose virtues her father instilled in her decried growing flowers for the luxury of decoration.

Yet the flower becomes fruit and seeds. It is an organ of reproduction.

In the aptly named house on Cherry Street in Cambridgeport, with her father away in Washington much of the time, the child Margaret slept with her mother and one or the other of the family's maids. Margaret's father was evidently home frequently enough to make his personal flower (Margaret's mother) blossom and bear further fruit. Other children, therefore, ultimately slept nearby in trundle beds. Margaret's mother had nine children, two of whom died young. In 1820, when Margaret was ten, her mother wrote to her husband: "I have long thought that the constant care of children narrowed the mind."

Margaret herself adored children, a maternal proclivity about which Jung has much to say. Margaret was devastated when Emerson lost little Waldo, and when Horace Greeley's son Pickie died. She herself had only the one child, Angelo (Nino). He was her flower, her blossom, her fruit.

D. *Personal Horoscope*

Margaret was born on May 23, 1810, under the sign of Gemini, the Twins. Whatever she did or did not know about astrological determinism, her insightfulness about

her own instincts caused her to write to James Freeman
Clarke: "I have often told you that I had two souls and they
seem to roll over one another in the most incomprehensi-
ble way. Taste and wishes point one way and I seem forced
the other."

> Cf. Ilya Chambertin, *Encyclopedia of Astrology* (1972):
> *Remember that Gemini is a double-bodied sign as its symbol,*
> *The Twins, implies. This inclines the native toward duality of*
> *nature. There is often a two way pull between differing, (in*
> *extreme cases, sharply opposed) sides of your nature.*

Though Margaret, believing in destiny, had once told
Thomas Hicks that their horoscopes were in some respects
the same, she does not seem to have become deeply
involved with astrological prediction. But Ilya Chambertin,
writing more than a hundred years after her death that
"Gemini duality is likely to make your love-life complex and
tangled" was not far from the mark. Margaret was in love,
after all, with both Samuel Gray Ward and Anna Barker,
who loved and married each other. A tangle, surely.

And when Chambertin suggests: "A note, Gemini. Your
morals are your own concern. But common sense should
warn you that a single slip will bring a hail of troubles crash-
ing down on you—with disastrous results!" his comments
could easily be referred to New England's response to the
news that Margaret was bringing a child, and only possibly a
husband, back home from Italy. Her putative marriage in
question, friends feared for her reputation and urged her to
stay abroad. Even Emerson thought it best.

Perhaps, to refer once again to a psychological source, Jung might be more helpful in dealing with Geminian duality than Freud. How did *anima* and *animus* reside together in Margaret's psyche? How did they, in turn, connect to her interest in androgyny? Was it through an androgynous, twinned, Geminian self that she found, even in middle age, a welcome retreat into Intellect, "for *there* in sight at least I am a man"?

Was her own sense of an inner split between Intellect and Feeling exacerbated by the mysterious proclivities signalled by her horoscope? Surely she found it hard to accommodate her intellect to the stereotypical expectations of women at that time. But her letters, more than a thousand of them, indicate such delicacy of feeling, such intuitive prescience, such warm affection and love for her fellow humans, combined with that intellect, that she seems to have been able to maintain Intellect and Feeling together, side by side, if not fully fused. Possibly, her twinned selves did not so much indicate a split as an addition, an extra self, each complete as well as completing. The equations often cited by nineteenth-century writers are of course too simplistically stated:

MALE=INTELLECT   FEMALE=FEELING

But Margaret, possessed of an inordinate amount of both, once said insightfully: "A man's ambition with a woman's heart—Tis an accursed lot."

3

John Denton, the Chairman of the English Department at Fitzwilliam College, a Harvard-trained authority on British nineteenth-century literature, wrote his dissertation on John Ruskin. He is a small, slight man, prone to bowties and tweed jackets, of a style almost defunct in academia in the '90s. His permanently unlit pipe, conversationally brandished, confirms the stereotypical nature of his academic persona. Hair starting to thin and grey at the temples, lips often pressed firmly together (on very rare occasions uplifted at the edges to simulate a smile) he is, at 52, weighed down by an academic heaviness of spirit that reinforces the institutional at the expense of the humane. Students can never get him to waive the rules, even for family emergencies like illness or death. Exams missed are exams missed. No makeups allowed. With the members of his department he exercises the same inflexibility.

Attendance at department meetings is required, even for those of us on leave, if we are (as I am) within geographical reach. So I am called, on the first Monday of every month, to one of these, and as I sit in the meeting room (a conference room just beside his office), I look around me.

There is nothing at all decorative in the room, not even a photograph. Walls are painted an unpleasant beige, as if to point up by some institutional mandate a neutrality at odds with the very individual personae gathered here. An overhead light, on this dull day, casts an unworldly clarity upon us, heightening what none of us would wish amplified.

Natasha Owens, a Women's Studies specialist, is tall and wiry, with straight black hair, cut very short. In this unflattering light, falling like some daemonic dust upon her face, I can see that her brand of feminism (possibly?) has led her to neglect her skin. No daily moisturizer. No creams of any kind. Wrinkles, perhaps only lightly etched, seem in this light to be *cut* into the surface of her skin, penetrating the countless layers of tissue that together comprise our flesh. Deep. Deep. If she doesn't relent, repent her uncompromising bias against beauty aids, she will look like a spider's web by the time she's 50. Natasha's Web. Sequel to Charlotte's.

Dressed as usual in running shoes and jeans, she smiles under her heavy glasses, producing still more wrinkles—those around the mouth, for which there are exercises, if you can remember to do them. These involve opening the mouth wide and tucking the upper lip in. Grotesque in the mirror, but worth doing.

Now she asks, as always, about my research, following this as usual with an invitation to lunch. I did once accept her invitation for a quick cup of coffee, but soon regretted it, since it quickly became evident that we disagreed about everything from Virginia Woolf to men and marriage. A militant lesbian, she would love to unseat John Denton from the chair, considering him not only inflexible but sexist. She spends much of her time trying to gather evidence of the latter from the women students. Since I am working on Margaret, she assumes my complicity to be a given.

Now that I have progressed in my research to a consideration of Margaret's adhesiveness, I realize that my dismissal of Natasha's attentions is shortsighted. Where else, in my acquaintance, could I find a better authority on same-sex love between women? On Margaret's adhesiveness? Though she has as yet made no advances to me, they lie before me, surely, in the future. This makes me a bit uneasy.

Now I find myself focused on her lipstickless lips, wondering what it would feel like to kiss them. No rough stubble as our faces rub together. No scratches from an unshaven chin. Would it be a tongue kiss? Would the tongue be different? What is the difference between engaging a male tongue and a female tongue? What of the breath? Is the breath more deliberately sweetened? Or is it by definition sweeter, more of *la différence*? Without moisturizer, is her skin more leathery? More male? But there are all sorts of products for men today. Including moisturizers. Does one woman without moisturizer equal one man with moisturizer? Could I do a skin experiment?

I am distracted from these ruminations by the entry of yet another member of the department—Margaretta Sinclair, who teaches creative writing. She has been around even longer than John Denton, who if he were indeed sexist would surely be disturbed by the large female constituency under his academic aegis. Margaretta has taught at the college for 35 years. So long that she received tenure before the current publication requirements were in place. Her publication credits, accordingly, are quite thin, consisting only of a few short stories published in small literary magazines out West, so small they are almost impossible to find—from places like Anigona, New Mexico and Wordsworth (no relation to the poet), Arizona. Her students, however, seem to blossom under her tutelage, and it is rumored that a novel, long in preparation, is nearing completion. Since this rumor has existed almost as long as Margaretta's service to the college, we cannot, of course, place too much store in it. But the fact of the matter is, Margaretta's position seems unassailable. She is here till death or retirement. The latter (no longer a legal requirement) unlikely.

The only other male member of the department now enters and sits beside me: Bill Lipton. Distinctive for his Don Juanish behavior, which democratically includes not only the seduction of his students, but his female colleagues as well. Though Bill Lipton rarely drinks tea, preferring mixes of vodka and cranberry juice, he is alleged to have inherited considerable wealth from a distant relation within the family. Not dependent on his salary for his livelihood, he clearly values his academic status, which in his mind seems to elevate his desirability far above that of the usual bachelor in a Boston condo. His ribald humour is in any case signaled by his natural affinity with the subject of his expertise: Boccaccio.

Bill Lipton has indicated some hope that my interest in Margaret does not preclude the possiblility of my interest in him. I have tried to be as prudent as possible in neither encouraging nor discouraging him, though unlike the proverbial Hollywood starlet, I have no intention of sleeping my way up. A full professor, he, along with John Denton and Margaretta Sinclair, will decide my fate. Natasha Owens, despite her campaign against John Denton, has not yet gathered enough evidence to unseat him, or indeed damage him in any way. Her own vote is a lesser one, since she is a tenured member of the Women's Studies department and teaches in the English department only as a visitor. But at the discretion of the others, her vote might be solicited. So I am politically at their mercy. And to some extent (at least with Natasha Owens and Bill Lipton), sexually as well.

The big question is: How will they take to a book about Margaret and love?

I glance about the room, absorbing John Denton's gesturing pipe, Natasha's dark, slim androgyny, Margaretta's frowzy clothes and frizzled graying hair, and Bill Lipton's lascivious eyes, peering at me like a mischievous satyr in a Bacchanal by Jordaens, round belly fed as much by gastronomic excess as by sexual lust. I wonder if I will soon be dangling from the end of my academic rope. I am not only being swallowed by Margaret. I am feasibly on the verge of academic suicide. Retreat might be possible if I leaven the book with enough intellectual fodder. But having devoted so much time and research to the love topic, I cannot so quickly shift to the lofty philosophical precincts of Transcendentalism. Of course I could argue that same-sex love is purer. Plato did. But I don't know how that will sit with Bill Lipton. And Natasha's vote, even were I to get—or earn—it, might not even be solicited by the department.

I hear John Denton asking if I will soon deliver my interim report. I hear my own voice speaking rather authoritatively about Margaret's translation of Eckermann's *Conversations with Goethe*. About her interest in the relationship of Bettina and Günderode, which ignites an echoing spark of interest from Natasha Owens. About Margaret's concept of intuition and its relation to the German ideal theories that presumably gave American Transcendentalism its name. About the irreplaceable loss in the shipwreck not only of her life, but of her volume on the Roman Republic.

I suppose I sound sufficiently erudite, but in truth, I am a coward. I don't admit where the full weight of my study will fall.

4

The A's (*Animus/Anima, Amativeness, Adhesiveness, Androgyny*) are in the red file. Red. The color of passion, of heart.

Jung might have said that Margaret had a strong dose of animus in her psyche:

> Woman is compensated by a masculine element and therefore her unconscious has, so to speak, a masculine imprint. This results in a considerable psychological difference between men and women, and accordingly I have called the projection-making factor in women the animus, which means mind or spirit. The animus corresponds to the paternal Logos just as the anima corresponds to the maternal Eros.

Remember the bust of Eros in the Hicks painting of Margaret. After her death, when Emerson wrote that her

friendships with women "were not unmingled with passion," he noted also that, though there had been "ebbs and
recoils from the other party," she ultimately grew more strict
and valued herself with her friends on having the tie "now
redeemed from all search after Eros."

Yet judging from her late liaison with Ossoli, Eros had not
been fully abandoned. And if, in Jungian terms, Eros was
maternal, even more so was the later Margaret, engrossed,
bewitched, enchanted by her infant Nino. Possessed, in fact,
by the Maternal Eros. But the Paternal Logos, (the animus)
remained strong in her. Was this *masculine imprint* (to use
Jung's terms) the factor that encouraged her passionate relationships with women? And was it also, reciprocally, her
masculine imprint that repeatedly doused male interest?

Even today, a woman with a fair dose of Logos (animus)
has to be careful in male company. After nearly 40 years of
feminism, after early pioneers like Simone de Beauvoir and
Betty Friedan, after the later development of the movement
in the subtle hands of such figures as Jane Gallop and
Griselda Pollock, after all the social changes that have been
effected: women firefighters, policewomen, army cadets—
after all that, men are still intimidated by intelligent women.

But picture Margaret, if you will, in the mid-nineteenth
century. Picture her holding forth on her hero Goethe, on
the rights of women, on Transcendental theories of intuition,
and imagine the glazed eyes of most men, even those on her
intellectual level, when she spoke. Spoke when?

One can imagine her ill-advisedly advancing her intellect
as dance conversation. Emerson, to his credit, called her con-

versation "the most entertaining in America." She herself immodestly knew this, stating that "a woman of tact and brilliancy, like me, has an undue advantage in conversation with men."

Did she gloat over her conversational one-upmanship? Hawthorne, most of all, seems to have been frightened by her. If he did, indeed, model Zenobia in *The Blithedale Romance* after Margaret (though there he also mentioned Margaret separately by name, and spoke glowingly of her as "one of the most gifted women of the age"), what did he mean when he wrote that Zenobia's mind was full of weeds? Yet Zenobia had lent his alter-ego, Miles Coverdale, George Sand's romances. As probably Margaret had Hawthorne.

It was surely Margaret he had in mind when he wrote of Zenobia, "Love had gone against her." Though Coverdale claims to take the feminist's part: "It is nonsense, and a miserable wrong—the result like so many others, of masculine egotism—that the success or failure of woman's existence should be made to depend wholly on the affections, and on one species of affection; while man has such a multitude of other chances," Hawthorne nonetheless wrote cruelly in his notebook after her death that Margaret "had not the charm of womanhood."

His conflicting feelings about Margaret are echoed by his feelings towards Melville. To neither of these figures—in essence androgynous—in whom masculine and feminine, anima and animus, amative and adhesive sentiments were so complexly interchanged, did he extend genuine understanding.

Perhaps, indeed, he was himself more of a mix than he was willing to admit. Margaret's life and persona ultimately upset him enough for him to negate her posthumously, and betray what she had considered a friendship. But, of course, Margaret had never offered him her love, and if we are to tease out his reasons for giving Priscilla in *The Blithedale Romance* Margaret's "partial closing of the eyes" and curved shoulders, and add to this Coverdale's confession at the very end that "I—I myself—was in love—with—Priscilla!" we are left with the provocative thought that maybe he was the one person to whom Margaret *should* have offered her love. Though probably, for all the reasons stated, not least his treatment of his wife, Sophia (made suitably cowed and passive after their marriage), he would have rejected Margaret as did all the others.

Like a nineteenth-century Jung, Margaret had claimed in "The Great Lawsuit—Man versus Men; Woman versus Women," (later expanded into her famous *Woman in the Nineteenth Century*), that male and female elements were "perpetually passing into one another. Fluid hardens to solid, solid rushes to fluid. There is no wholly masculine man, no purely feminine woman." This probably characterized and qualified her amative/adhesiveness. Her first love, at the age of eight, was a visiting Englishwoman, Ellen Kilshaw, of whom she wrote, "It was my first real interest in my kind, and it engrossed me wholly."

It seems significant that Ellen Kilshaw came to New England from Europe. Was this the beginning of the

Jamesian theme of cultivated Europe versus repressed and raw America that Margaret's life ultimately acted out? She died returning home from Italy. Europe had certainly changed her. Was it possible that, as some suggested (given the reluctance of many of her friends to deal with a *new* Margaret, an only *possibly* married Margaret, with an Italian appendage and a hardly known-about child), she really could not go home again?

Can we distinguish, albeit arbitrarily, between Margaret's amativeness and her adhesiveness? Could we, for the sake of argument or clarity, speak of her amativeness with men, her adhesiveness with women? Amativeness in nineteenth-century phrenological terms, was heterosexual. Adhesiveness was generally characterized as comradely affection between persons of the same sex. The element of sexuality in adhesiveness was consistently occluded by those who practiced it, even by such a clear practitioner as Whitman in the Calamus poems. Elevated by noble ideas of friendship and spiritual sentiment, so-called Boston marriages or romantic friendships between women were touted as being above the flesh. If we accept that it is hard to divine the physical or erotic nature of Margaret's relationships, and if we assume, without evidence to the contrary, that she was a virgin until her encounter with Ossoli, we still find ourselves with the problem of her passion, of her involvement with Eros, of her heart's amativeness and adhesiveness, and more important, of the slippage between them. Can we chart at least some of her relationships?

AMATIVE	ADHESIVE
George Davis	Ellen Kilshaw
James Freeman Clarke	Eliza Farrar
Samuel Gray Ward	Anna Barker
Ralph Waldo Emerson	Caroline Sturgis
James Nathan	
Giovanni Ossoli	
Adam Mickiewicz	
Thomas Hicks	

Such a listing has the advantage also of drawing us onto a short tour of some of Margaret's loves.

GEORGE DAVIS: An early love. Distant cousin. Harvard student of the class of 1829 who shared and encouraged Margaret's intellectual interests. After graduation from Harvard, he left to read law in Greenfield and lessened his contact with her, partly perhaps because he disagreed with her liberated stance on religion. She felt dropped. Rejected. Denying that she had felt more than an attachment for him, she ultimately (1831) wrote to him: "I feel that but for you I should be free at last in the common or worldly sense of the word. You are the only person who can appreciate my true self. . . ."

Margaret's attachment to George Davis is instructive insofar as she expected more from him than he could deliver. She considered herself straightforward. She considered him insincere. It was the beginning of a pattern, in which she made herself vulnerable, expressed deep feelings, and expected, indeed demanded, like treatment. In this instance, when she didn't receive it, she fell into what seems to have been a clinical depression, oversleeping around the clock, without access, in that pre-modern age, to either Prozac or Lithium.

JAMES FREEMAN CLARKE: Davis's close friend and Harvard classmate. Clarke tried to act as mediator between Davis and Margaret and also as Margaret's intellectual mentor and supporter, encouraging her to begin her life-long work on Goethe. She rewarded him by trying to rupture his amative relationship with Elizabeth Randall, whom she claimed was "unsuited" to him. Clarke, remaining a friend, ultimately tried to distance himself and wrote to her, "Do not determine that if we are not all to each other we shall be nothing." But Margaret, voracious Margaret, wanted all, always, and there is evidence that years later she expected the same return of her affections from his brother William.

ELIZA FARRAR: An early mentor, who took her under wing and tried to smooth off the rough social edges that led Margaret later to describe herself at nineteen as "the most intolerable girl that ever took a seat in a drawing room." Had she, indeed, been spouting Goethe in social situations instead of the expected pretty feminine chatter? She had long determined that, since her complexion had grown in adolescence suddenly florid, she would be "bright and ugly."

Probably Margaret never saw herself as beautiful. But judging from ANONYMOUS's daguerreotype, I see something of Bette Davis in the bulge of her downcast eyes. Was she anything like Bette in her swagger and arrogance? Arrogant because of Mind?

I am distracted by the phone. Natasha Owens is calling and inviting me to lunch. Since I have just begun to consider the adhesiveness problem I am happy now to accept her invitation. She gives me the address: 275 Commonwealth Avenue. We agree to meet in about an hour. I put aside the red folder, hoping that lunch will be instructive. What are my feelings? Do I want to attract her? To what purposeful end? I hesitate over what to wear, and settle on jeans and a white sweater. I know Natasha Owens will be wearing jeans as always.

5

Commonwealth Avenue's high-stooped nineteenth-century terrace houses are so London-like they satisfy whatever latent Anglophilia lurks within me. Once inside, I climb one flight up to her floor-through with anticipation. Before, I was a bit afraid of Natasha's interest. Now, I am motivated by something stronger than fear: the possibility of understanding adhesiveness. Is my interest thoroughly scholarly and objective? I suppose there is some sexual curiosity mixed in. What would a romantic friendship with another woman be like? A Boston (fittingly for the city in which I find myself) marriage.

Natasha meets me at the door. Dressed as predicted in jeans and running shoes. Topped today with a black silk shirt. In the dimness of the hallway, I am mainly conscious of her sparkling eyes, wrinkles forgotten. I enter a book-lined room, not unlike my own, but better tended. Very clean. Very precise.

Each object carefully highlighted:

A blue vase here, a small, bronze sculpture there.

A round white ceramic lamp with a wide shade beside a black couch.

A red-patterned Oriental rug on the floor.

All these register because they have been separated out. In my apartment, books, papers, vases, lamps, art, jostle so indiscriminately against one another, they glom together. A sticky mass of clutter.

So she is orderly. I now know that. My sense of her orderliness somehow mitigates my anxiety about her adhesiveness. How adhesive anyway is she? Sticky again then, despite the order. Would our bodies stick together? Men and women could stick more easily because they have parts made to fit. The pole and the hole. What sensible God figured that out?

Now Natasha gives me a slight hug and a peck on the cheek. Innocent enough, but I am still wary. Two courses of action are open to me:

1. I can simply ask her, frankly, if as a lesbian she might explain her activities so that I might better understand Margaret's same-sex affections.
2. I can participate and learn by doing.

I decide to let her actions be my guide. We chat for a while about the department. She has not yet found enough evidence that John Denton acted with sexual bias against his female students. But she is still hopeful.

We sit down to eat. She has set the small rectangular table neatly. Has prepared salads. Has made tea. Now she asks about Margaret. Good. Maybe I can proceed with Plan One.

For a while we simply consume our food. I pay careful attention to the salad: bibb lettuce, tomatoes on the vine, tuna, anchovies, black olives, croutons, hard-boiled eggs, all with balsamic dressing. A salade niçoise, in effect. Does that tell me anything? It could have been Spam. So, she is not only orderly, she is also somewhat domestic. The olives are large, fresh and juicy. I savor them on my tongue. I make some attempt at pertinent conversation to advance my cause—my Margaret-cause.

ANGELICA: I think she might have been bisexual.

NATASHA: Was she? I do know she was one of the earliest American feminists.

ANGELICA: In the nineteenth century they called same-sex relationships adhesive.

NATASHA: Sticky?

ANGELICA: I guess so. (*I stifle a nervous giggle. I want to seem laid back.*)

NATASHA: Have you ever had one?

ANGELICA: One what?

NATASHA: An adhesive relationship.

ANGELICA: I'm not sure I know exactly what it involves.

NATASHA (*rising from her chair, having left three lettuce leaves and a slice of tomato on her plate, approaching my end of the table*): Let me show you.

She is quick. Very quick. Before I realize what is happening she has pushed me back, one hand on my neck, the other on my breast. Which breast? I'm not quite sure. Left or right doesn't matter. She has landed on my breast and is now thrusting her tongue into my mouth. I am trying to the best of my capacity to cope. Am I repelled? Curious? Simply taken unawares? I am trying to analyze my feelings before I terminate the kiss. Her tongue moves around in my mouth. Her breath is Listerine-sweet, against the more piquant residue of olive taste. Her skin is soft. From this angle, I cannot see her wrinkles. The nipple of my breast starts to respond. I push her away.

NATASHA (*looking hurt*): You know I'm attracted to you. You're working on Margaret. You must have feminist instincts.

ANGELICA: All feminist instincts are not sexual.

NATASHA: They could be. Just follow them to their logical conclusion. Women are better.

ANGELICA (*rising from my chair*): Thanks for the lunch. (*I still have six lettuce leaves, two slices of tomato and one-half of a hard-boiled egg on my plate.*)

NATASHA (*keeping her seat*): Think about it.

ANGELICA (*nearing the door*): And thanks for the enlightenment.

NATASHA (*still seated, laughing now*): I'll light your fire any time.

She is not angry. Nor am I. I exit, feeling as if we part still friends, though I'm not sure what I've learned. This was just

a pass. Just sexual. Margaret's loves, adhesive or not, were
something much more.

Later, at home, I rifle once more through the red folder.
Always with Margaret it is hard to know where to begin.
Every layer leads to another. Facts pile on facts, texts on
texts. So much material has already been published, in addition to the unpublished bits and pieces of manuscript I am
unearthing in Houghton. In some ways, it is as if I could
reconstruct her life day by day. Yet that is almost too much,
would take a lifetime in itself to do. *My* lifetime. I am not
quite willing to go that far. I would have to get as close as
possible to reexperiencing all of her living. No. I must sift.
Synthesize. And through it all, I am trying to divine what
was *not* written, the words that went out into the air, the
thoughts never recorded, the tastes, smells, and feelings that
even she did not always understand or acknowledge.

I am searching for her life-blood and breath, and out of
all that, for some kind of truth. An odd thing to do at the
end of the twentieth century, when Truth (a nineteenth-
century term) is no longer something many scholars in a
post-Foucault world believe in. Foucault wanted to kill
Sartre and did a good job of it. He also killed a lot of little
boys in the bathhouses he attended while knowingly dying
of AIDS. Was that adhesiveness? How lethal was adhesiveness in the nineteenth century?

It was, of course, free of the AIDS virus. But among men,
at least, it could be socially quite lethal; viz. Oscar Wilde who
went to prison for it because he loved Lord Douglas, and

who ultimately died at the address on the Rue des Beaux Arts in Paris now known to rock stars as "L'Hotel."

But Margaret's adhesiveness was never frowned on, not even by Emerson who fully recognized her passion. And Truth, nineteenth-century Truth, was one of Margaret's greatest ideals. Is it Truth or truths I am chasing as I pursue the Margaret-Ghost? The relativity of truth is something I would love to hear the Margaret-Ghost debate with the Foucault-Ghost.

6

It's hard to tell how much Margaret read of Eliza Farrar's 1836 *The Young Lady's Friend*, but it was Farrar's book that offered the model for behavior with other women:

> All kissing and caressing of your female friends should be kept for your hours of privacy, and never indulged in before gentlemen.

Now what was that all about? An assumption, surely, that kissing and caressing went on between women, and was subject to certain interpretations. A license for intimacy in private behavior? Affection? Eroticism? How far could it, did it go, towards "surpassing the love of men," as one recent book on the subject would have it.

It is altogether likely that Margaret's relation with Eliza

Farrar remained within the simple bounds of friendship, though even at age eight her proclamation of love for Ellen Kilshaw seemed to merge amativeness and adhesiveness: "I LOVE ELLEN MORE THAN MY LIFE." Eliza Farrar, however, established for Margaret a pattern of friendships with women that continued throughout her life, a support system of sisters readily recognizable today, both in and out of feminist circles. Eliza also gave Margaret an introduction to her young cousin, Anna Barker, who became one of the great "adhesive" loves of Margaret's life, became, in Margaret's poems to her, her "heart's fancy" and "fancy's love." Margaret kept the relationship going as a romantic love, in her own mind at least, for ten years. At the same time, she began to develop a strong attachment to Samuel Gray Ward, whom she ultimately chided (in tones familiar to us by now) for not seeing as much of her as before: "... if you love me as I deserve to be loved, you cannot dispense with seeing me ... We knew long ago that age, position and pursuits being so different, nothing but love bound us together and it must not be my love alone that binds us."

Anna Barker! Even Emerson found her beautiful. Henry Inman, one of the most popular and stylish portraitists of the time, did a soft, Lawrence-like painting of her at 17, shortly before she met Margaret. Later, Hiram Powers did a stunning marble bust of her. Wasn't it inevitable that Sam Ward, Margaret's "Raffaello," should also fall in love with Anna Barker? How was this potential ménage à trois to be resolved?

When puritan sentiment saw to it that Anna and Sam

were duly married, Margaret's twin souls were each betrayed in both their amative and adhesive guises.

Margaret had seen Anna as Récamier to her own de Staël. Though Margaret has been likened to de Staël's fictional heroine Corinne, de Staël herself was a strange model for her. Margaret decried de Staël's lifestyle: "While she was instructing you as a mind, she wished to be admired as a woman . . . her intellect . . . fed on flattery, was tainted and flawed." Still, she found de Staël a strong intellectual paradigm. Benjamin Constant, with whom de Staël had a relationship for about 13 years, described her as "a little too stout to be graceful . . ." but "irresistibly seductive as soon as she spoke and gestured. Her mind, the most far ranging that any woman (and perhaps any man) has ever had, showed more strength than grace in intellectual matters . . . Within an hour she had secured over me the greatest sway that a woman can gain over a man. I decided to settle near her, and soon I was living in her house. I spent the whole winter telling her of my love."

De Staël was, of course, infinitely more sophisticated and cosmopolitan than Margaret in her New England phase, with a large number of male objects of her very erotic amativeness and few pretexts of simple friendship. Her relation to Juliette Récamier (picture Récamier in David's classic portrait, reclining on her chaise in her ubiquitous white gown) was adhesively amative. Récamier loyally followed de Staël into exile when Napoleon banished her from Paris in 1803. Later, in a strange twist, not so far removed from Margaret's relation to Anna Barker and Sam Ward, Constant fell in love with

Récamier, who seems to have managed to stay technically virginal throughout her long-standing marriage to Jacques Récamier from the age of 16 on, ultimately relinquishing her virginity to become Chateaubriand's mistress at the age of 42, and dying in Italy in 1849, a year before Margaret.

It was of Anna Barker as her Récamier that Margaret wrote so famously: "It is so true that a woman may be in love with a woman and a man with a man." She likened it to the "same love that we shall feel when we are angels" and claimed it was regulated "by the same law as that of love between persons of different sexes, only it is purely intellectual and spiritual, unprofaned by any mixture of lower instincts." So she claimed. But in the same journal entry she spoke of "that night when she leaned on me and her eyes were such a deep violet blue, so like night . . . and we both felt such a strange mystic thrill and knew what we had never known before."

After Anna and Sam were married, Margaret noted in her journal that "Sam was away, and I slept with Anna the first time for two years . . . I took pleasure in sleeping on Sam's pillow. . . ."

Sam's pillow! Slept how? Chastely? Like an adolescent pillow party today? Are pillow parties indeed chaste? Is a mystic thrill chaste? Was St. Teresa, as portrayed by Bernini in ecstasy in the Church of Santa Maria della Vittoria in Rome, was St. Teresa's mystic thrill chaste? I think not. I think it was gloriously orgasmic. And what about the knowledge they "had never known before?" Is it prurient to ask these questions about Margaret's love-life? Without the answers, I am hard put to write about her. Love was as central to her as Logos. Eros and Logos went hand in hand.

Margaret's amative/adhesiveness extended to other women as well. To Caroline Sturgis, with whom she had a mysterious argument at Nahant, presumably because Sturgis would not avow her love. Sturgis, the daughter of a sea captain, had an emotionally unstable mother, and was still suffering from her family's difficulties when she met Margaret in 1836 at the age of fifteen. Their relationship lasted as a mixture of amativeness and adhesiveness for the next eight years, and thereafter as a less emotionally loaded friendship until Margaret's death. If Caroline (Cary) looked to Margaret in any way as a substitute for her mother, Margaret's feelings for her were decidedly more romantic.

> No doubt [she wrote in 1839] I was somewhat pained by your want of affection towards me while in Boston, but I did not dislike you, on the contrary I loved you as much as was consistent with the crowded, wearied state of my mind at that time . . . I could not seriously think there was any danger of your ceasing to love me. There is so much in me that you do not yet know and have faculties to apprehend that you will not be able, I believe, to get free of me for some years.

That last could apply to me as well. What kind of relationship do I have with the Margaret-Ghost? I feel, having taken her on, that I will not get free of her for years. Surely not soon enough for the academic timetable. Untenured professors are, as they say, "on the clock." We have seven years to prove ourselves, by the publication of at least one *magnum opus* (though preferably two). If not, no matter how fine we are as teachers, how good our scholarship, quantity outranks quality. Out we go, into the wide, wide world, away from the sheltering arms of the college, which after all pays us to read and write. Where else could we find such welcome subsidy? Is it true that all academics are perennial students, unwilling to leave the library for the so-called real world of business or even of the professions? Doctor, lawyer, Indian chief. Margaret had such great compassion for the Indians who were slowly succumbing to nationally self-justified genocide. I haven't yet factored in her compassion. There are just so many things to factor in with Margaret.

She was right. There is "so much in her that I do not yet know." I will not get free of her for years. And much as it intrigues me, the college surely does not want a book on Margaret's love-life. What would they prefer? I know quite well.

MARGARET AS FEMINIST,
holding her famous "Conversations" to elevate the women of the Boston area. Tending to the prostitutes of New York City.

MARGARET AS TRANSCENDENTALIST,
challenging even Emerson in intellectual discourse.

MARGARET AS WAR CORRESPONDENT,
reporting from Italy on the 1848 war.

MARGARET AS EXPATRIATE,
realizing American dreams of Europe.

MARGARET AS CRITIC,
of both art and literature.

MARGARET AS POET,
a little known facet of her extraordinary mind.

MARGARET AS FICTIONAL HEROINE,
inspiring both Hawthorne and James.

Of course, she was all of these, and I might touch on
some of them in my study. But love was as central to her as
intellect. Please understand. I am not writing tabloid gossip.
I am only trying to get at Margaret's mystery. It cannot be
punctured except through love, for LOVE (capitalized) was
what she really sought. When she wrote to Cary, "I also love
you, and, probably, no other person you know could be so
much to you as I, not withstanding all my shortcomings,"
Anna Barker was already in the picture. Anna must have
posed a serious challenge to Margaret's feelings for Cary, for
on another occasion Margaret wrote:

> My dear Caroline,
> Your letter, for which I had often wished in calmer days,
> arrived nearly a week ago in the very first days of Anna.
> At that time I could not even read it—I could not think of
> our relation, so filled was I so intoxicated, so uplifted by
> that eldest and divinest love . . . Even yet I cannot think of

you . . . I cannot tell you what I shall think or feel . . . I loved you, Caroline, with truth and nobleness. I counted to love you much more, I thought there was a firm foundation for future years. In this hour, when my being is more filled and answered than ever before, when my beloved has returned to transcend in every way not only my hope, but my imagination, I will tell you that I once looked forward to the time when you might hold as high a place in my life as she . . . How this hope was turned sickly, how deeply it was wounded you know not yet, you do not fully understand what you did or what passed in my mind . . . I will own that in no sacred solitary woodland walk, in no hour of moonlight love had I been able to feel that that hope could recover from its wound.

What on earth had Cary done? Surely nothing as shattering as Anna Barker's ultimate defection in marrying a man Margaret also loved. What did she expect of a lover, a loved one? What did she believe was love? This love business is wearing on me. But I am determined to follow it through. I am convinced it is the KEY TO MARGARET! I will find in it not only the key to Margaret, but somehow, a key to my own feelings. Perhaps those of other women as well.

Am I being too ambitious? Am I looking, in the almost twenty-first century, for universal truths? Those truths, lacking an absolute, that Foucault would negate? Do I dare at this point in the development of scholarly opinion to oppose truth's relativity? To claim that Truth in the nineteenth-century sense might still have some value? That there are still some absolutes, almost a hundred years after Einstein and Relativity? I can feel the floor boards under my feet as I write. I am not whizzing into space on a time-space continuum. I am still here, in some kind of Newtonian time. Even Berkeley was willing to admit that there was common-sense knowledge that could preempt Mind. Is knowledge about love common sense knowledge? Instinctual? Programmed into us as into the birds and bees, who are hardly politically correct, and don't give a damn about Foucault?

I reexamine my list of amatives. Did Margaret have any qualms about her relation with Emerson? She managed to reduce Lidian to tears when she visited the red room in the house at Concord. She was quite blithe, almost cruel about Lidian. Emerson's own feelings for Lidian could also be questioned. Though his year-and-a-half marriage to Ellen Tucker seems to have remained a romantic idyll in his mind, after he married Lidian he was more vocal about the difficulties and problems of the married state.

He considered the self-reliant soul more important than the united souls of a husband and wife. Marriage, he claimed, "is not ideal but empirical. It is not in the plan or prospect of the soul, this fast union of one to one—the soul is alone and creates these images of itself . . . To a strong mind therefore the griefs incident to every earthly marriage are the less . . . The Universe is his bride." (Later, after Margaret declared, "I accept the Universe," Carlyle remarked famously, "She'd better.") With the Universe as Emerson's bride, Lidian had every right to complain that their union was not sufficiently "intimate."

INTIMATE. That word again. In the nineteenth century, as opposed to our own, it could readily have meant an intimate union of soul or spirit. Emerson had had that union with Ellen Tucker. Not only did he open her coffin 13 months after her death, he readily acceded to Lidian's generous but ill-thought-out suggestion that he name his daughter by Lidian for Ellen. So she survived into his next marriage. (There was, of course, a family history of opening coffins—a tradition, we might almost say. Ralph Waldo's father had exhumed his own father, presumably to look at him, 18 years after his death. And 15 years after little Waldo's death, Emerson dug *him* up. It is even claimed that Ellen was exhumed again 25 years later).

The motivations behind this seemingly genetically inspired necrophilia remain inexplicable. Should Lidian have been jealous of Ellen's ghost? After the birth of the daughter named Ellen, Lidian had to cope not only with this ghost-by-name in the family, but with the Margaret-Ghost in the flesh. With Margaret's visits. With Margaret and Emerson's lifelong friendship.

Actually, a mysterious friendship, in which the presence of each so disturbed the other. When little Waldo was alive, happily carrying notes between them, within the same house on Cambridge Turnpike in Concord where Margaret stayed in the red room, Emerson found Margaret so forceful, he often felt he had to "stand from under." Margaret found him too cold, and liked to visit his library when he was "out of it. It seems a sacred place." But in the flesh, in his presence, "I cannot receive you, and you cannot give yourself; it does not profit." After the child Waldo's death, however, she did visit him in the library "late in the evening. Then I go knock at the library door, and we have our long word walk through the growths of things with glimmers of light from the causes of things." She found him hard to know, "the subtle Greek." He, for his part, wrote about "these strange, cold-warm, active-repelling conversations with Margaret . . . whom I freeze, & who freezes me to silence."

The accusations of his coldness were, of course, part of Margaret's pattern in relationships. Emerson was, by nature, aloof, yet she made him wryly self-conscious about his distancing, and he wrote to her about his awkwardness in loving his friends: "My love reacts on me like the recoiling gun; it is pain . . . I was going to add something concerning the capacity to love of this reputed icicle, but the words would tell nothing, and we shall certainly pass at last with each other for what we are." The reputed icicle, in turn, was ambivalent about Margaret, who with her brilliance, her "riches still unknown and . . . unknowable" must have baffled and intrigued him, even as he treated Lidian like a housekeeper.

The ambivalence continued after her death. We can see it in his comments about her in the memoir he was so instrumental in publishing, in which passages from her papers were deleted and censored since it was meant for public reading. He was more effusive in private, in his own journal entry of 1843 where he praised her "silver eloquence": "She rose before me at times into heroical & godlike regions, and I could remember no superior women, but thought of Ceres, Minerva, Proserpine, and the august ideal forms of the

Foreworld. She said that no man gave such invitation to her mind as to tempt her to a full expression . . . " In the Journal, too, he had written:

> You would have me love you. What shall I love? Your body? The supposition disgusts you. . . . [He found Margaret] a being of unsettled rank in the Universe. So proud & presumptuous yet so meek, so worldly and artificial & with keenest sense & taste for all pleasures of luxurious society, yet living more than any other for long periods in a trance of religious sentiment; a person who according to her own account of herself, expects everything for herself from the Universe . . . [But he also felt that] a highly endowed man with good intellect & good conscience is a Man-woman & does not so much need the complement of Woman to his being, as another. Hence his relations to the sex are somewhat dislocated & unsatisfactory. He asks in Woman, sometimes the Woman, sometimes the Man.

What did he ask of Margaret? Mostly he asked for the man. Women, even women like Lidian (who had hardly been blessed with Margaret's intellectual gifts) perplexed him. "Few women," he noted in his journal, "are sane." Earlier he had confided to those pages that "women generally have weak wills, sharply expressed perhaps, but capricious, unstable. When the will is strong we inevitably respect it, in man or woman." Margaret's will, clearly, was something he *had* to respect.

But despite his devotion to Margaret, Emerson's comments on women are ambiguous throughout his journals, and sometimes betray a sexism of which he would have found himself guiltless.

"Love," he claimed, was "necessary to the righting the estate of woman in this world. Otherwise nature itself seems to be in conspiracy against her dignity & welfare; for the cultivated, high thoughted, beauty-loving, saintly woman finds herself unconsciously desired for her sex. . . ." Though he declared that "we are not very much to blame for our bad marriages. We live amid hallucinations & illusions, & this especial trap is laid for us to trip up our feet with & all are tripped up, first or last . . . ," he also felt that women needed not only the loving estate of marriage, if it could indeed be achieved, but money. "Society lives on the system of money and woman comes at money & money's worth through compliment. I should not dare to be a woman . . . What is she not expected to do & suffer for some invitation to strawberries and cream."

After Margaret's death, as he read through her papers for the memoir, he noted: "The unlooked for trait in all these journals to me is the Woman, poor woman; they are all hysterical. She is bewailing her virginity and languishing for a husband." Poor Margaret. Even Emerson took the male view that a woman needed marriage and essentially *a good fuck* to find fulfillment.

As her unparalleled conversation, her "fine, generous, vinous, inspiring, eloquent" talking receded from his presence with her absence from his "audience," he found that her writing "did not outlive her influence." He admitted, however, that he loved her wit. Though initially her quickly blinking eyes disconcerted him, he soon found them swimming with "fun and drollness, and the very tides of joy and abundant life." His Aunt Mary Moody Emerson, who like Emily Dickinson always wore white, slept in a shroud and was rumoured also to sleep in a coffinlike bed (signaling a family predilection for coffins that must have encouraged the practice of exhumation) didn't think Margaret a good influence on him. But Emerson was too stuffy to be seriously led astray. At most, Margaret might have lightened his moods. (He *complained*, in fact, that she made him laugh.) Yet we *hear* of her wit more than we have evidence of it.

In her writings, and even in her letters, there is a seriousness and often a profundity that suggests she knew her time was short. Of love, of course, she wrote at length, though the copiousness of her writings and observations on the subject make her meaning even harder to decipher. She wrote so often about rejected love. Unrequited love. Was her compassion for the outsider, the marginalized, the Other, an empathy charged with her own situation? She was not only Other as a woman. She was Other as a *rejected* woman. From Emerson, she claimed intellectual understanding and parity, yet for all his admiration, he still saw her as Woman, complete with his caveats. But if Emerson froze her, she froze him, too. "To silence." She could match him, even in temperature. Did they touch down to zero?

7

The college has asked me for an interim report on my progress. What am I to tell them? That I am stuck in the quagmire of the Margaret-Ghost? That her loves are obsessing me? That only through her sense of love can I get at Margaret herself? And only if I get at her, really get *to* her, can I justify still another academic contribution to the Margaret industry. I want to flesh out the Ghost, as a woman, as a person. Gender distinctions are a problem. Margaret fought them as best she could. All her feminism was a protest against the arbitrary classifications of gender, at the same time that she celebrated Woman. Was she not really celebrating the Androgyne? An androgynous ideal, as I think of it, seems appropriate for a Geminian persona.

Coleridge, quoted by Carolyn Heilbrun, wrote in a comment not unlike Emerson's, that "A great mind must be androgynous." According to Heilbrun too, boy and girl twins

were "each endowed at birth with the experience of androgyny." Heilbrun traces zodiacal iconography into the thir-
teenth century, when opposite-sex twins were depicted on
the relief sculptures of Amiens. A boy and girl Gemini. Two
selves in one. An androgyne.

I set aside the red folder I am working on and leave the tall-
ceilinged studio I am renting on Dartmouth Street to walk
the streets of Cambridge as young Margaret might have
done, ending at Houghton Library, where I continue to
peruse Margaret's papers.

I am deep into them when I become annoyingly aware
of a presence. I have just been puzzling out a thought—I
don't dare call it an insight—about Margaret's sense of herself as a desirable (or undesirable) woman in her relationship
with James Nathan. The presence, or my awareness of it, dis-
perses the thought, pushes it out of my head, and I cannot
retrieve it. I am doubly irritated, then curious about the force
of a presence that can achieve such a result. He has not said
anything, but is sitting at the next desk. Has he been watching me? He is not doing so now. He seems engrossed in his
own work. Then what disturbed my concentration?

I've seen him in the library before. Tall, slender—very
close to bony—with a straight rather sensitive nose a bit
bumpy at the bridge, thin, but not ungenerous lips that quirk
up at one end, giving him a paradoxically jaunty look that
remains afterward in memory almost like the Cheshire cat's
grin. His darkish hair seems always to fall into his eyes,
necessitating a rather constant, not unrhythmic correctional

brush of the hand. Not quite Jeremy Irons, but then, not so unlike. I've always found Jeremy Irons a rather attractive specimen. So the Irons-ish presence absorbs me for a while. Long enough for him to look up and see me watching him. I look back at my own pile of papers. (A common enough ritual for men and women who find each other attractive and must then find a way to meet.)

Also, the library is fair ground. Not a bar. Not even *just* a library. The *Houghton* Library.

Filled with cultural rarities, an interest in which signals a certain elevated level of intellectual curiosity, if not status. It's a testament to our budding sense of friendship and comradery that when I look up again we both speak at once:

—How's it going? Then simultaneously:

—Coffee break?

In the silence of the library there is simply the sound of our chairs being pushed back. A slight skid. The rustle of our bodies rising. We leave our respective papers sitting on the desks with the legitimate expectation of becoming important to us again, books opened, folios only half closed, papers splayed irregularly across their supporting wooden surfaces. Even the chairs are somewhat askew.

Over a cup of decaf (never trust caffeine, no matter how early in the day) I learn that he is a Melville scholar, writing the book that will earn *him* tenure in the English department at Harvard. We are both, so to speak, in the same boat (no Melvillian pun intended), each of us feeling a bit oarless at the moment.

He asks if I am a man-hating feminist. A nearly unforgivable query for a presumably enlightened Harvard professor. (Provoked often enough, I regret to say, by my commitment to Margaret.) Were it not for that Jeremy Irons air, I would pull back right now. But his presence has something magnetic about it. Margaret, I feel, would understand, since her own concern with magnetism drew a considerable amount of criticism.

—Are you opposed to intelligent women?

—Only those opposed to men

—I'm not opposed to men.

—Fine. How about dinner?

We are walking and talking along the Charles, with the golden dome of the State House across the river lighting the sky. There are some parts of the Charles, I am told, that feel like the Seine, for all that Boston is not Paris. At this moment, I feel the way the few Frenchmen I have met have made me feel—desirable. Why desire, or being desired, should make me hungry I cannot explain, but with the decaf and muffins long gone, I am suddenly famished. Just as suddenly, I notice that my new friend, James Apthorp, has blue eyes. Only later do I remember that James Nathan, too, had blue eyes. Yet James Apthorp is not—like Nathan—a German Jew, but rather a New Englander, born and bred, with a family history that traces back to eighteenth-century Boston. For some inexplicable reason I decide that he might have genealogical ties to Margaret, which pleases me, since I have none of my own.

A native New Yorker, I've always wished I were a New Englander. I've always wanted a firmer connection to an American past dominated by WASP culture. Not because of the snobby country clubs to which I probably have no access, but because of the connection to the literature, the art, the philosophy. I want a connection to Jonathan Edwards, whose essay on spiders has always fascinated me.

My own family history includes some Viennese Jews who supplied the Buchbinder name that my father changed to Bookbinder. The Angelica comes from my mother's Italian Catholic side, as do my dark hair and coloring. All part of the immigrant wave of the late nineteenth century. But James's background is like Margaret's, receding far back into a puritan past. Margaret's puritanism, as a background for her love-life, is something I intend to research. My new friend offers a practical route to such knowledge, a vicarious connection with Margaret's heritage through the medium of our intellectual discourse. Even his own topic will help, since he is presently researching Melville's relationship with Hawthorne.

ANGELICA: He was adhesive, wasn't he?

JAMES: You mean like Whitman? Yes, I guess so. Judging from the episode with Queequeg in bed, as well. Of course, he was *plagued* by women.

ANGELICA: Plagued?

JAMES: His wife, mother, sisters. He had to lock them out with a big key while he wrote *Moby-Dick*.

ANGELICA: So that's why it's such a *man's* book!

(James Apthorp's eyes turn slightly gray.)

JAMES: They drove him nuts. He evicted them while he chased the Big Whale.

ANGELICA: The male/female thing in the nineteenth century is hard to unravel.

(His eyes darken further.)

JAMES: It's still hard to unravel.

8

N *is for Nathan*: the James Nathan folder is purple, for spirit. Margaret would have wanted it that way.

She had always felt alone. She had told Emerson that she knew she would want some hand to hold, but was glad she was not in the kind of non-marriages that surrounded her. She had written in "The Great Lawsuit":

> A great majority of societies and individuals are still doubtful whether earthly marriage is to be a union of souls, or merely a contract of convenience and utility... In our country the woman looks for a "smart but kind" husband, the man for a "capable, sweet-tempered" wife. The man furnishes the house, the woman regulates it ... The wife praises her husband as a "good provider," the husband in return compliments her as a "capital housekeeper."

Apt still, towards the end of the twentieth century. But liberated women today, and there are, after all, now many of them, would understand her visionary dream looking forward to "a female Newton, and a male Syren ... I would have woman lay aside all thought, such as she habitually cherishes, of being taught and led by men ... I would have her free from compromise, from complaisance, from helplessness, because I would have her good enough and strong enough to love one and all beings, from the fulness, not the poverty of being."

In *Woman in the Nineteenth Century* she again stated: "What woman needs is not as a woman to act or rule, but as a nature to grow, as an intellect to discern, as a soul to live freely, and unimpeded to unfold such powers as were given her when we left our common home."

She awaited the day:

> ... when inward and outward freedom for woman as much as for man shall be acknowledged as a right, not yielded as a concession. As the friend of the negro assumes that one man cannot, by right, hold another in bondage, so should the friend of woman assume that man cannot, by right, lay even well-meant restrictions on woman ... Let it not be said, wherever there is energy or creative genius, "she has a masculine mind."

Yet only two years after conceiving of "The Great Lawsuit," when James Nathan's attentions rain upon her, she is needy as a plant in the Texas sun (fitting, in the months preceding the Texas annexation she so opposed).

She has accepted Horace Greeley's invitation to move to New York and write for the *New-York Daily Tribune*. She has moved in with Greeley and his family at their home in Turtle Bay, near the old Boston Road at 49th Street, with the Third Avenue stage nearby.

Greeley's wife Molly, at first her supporter and mentor, then feasibly jealous of the Great Margaret, sets a background for the erstwhile lovers, appearing in Margaret's almost daily letters to Nathan as "our friend," at once co-conspirator for their contrived liaisons ("Meet me when I walk down to Wall St., I shall be out on Bowling Green at a quarter past ten") and disgruntled onlooker.

It is still inconceivable that Margaret Fuller, surely the most erudite woman on the North American continent in 1845, the year in which *Woman in the Nineteenth Century* is published, could have been such a dope about James Nathan, but such are the facts. For five months of that year, while he was present in New York, and for fully a year after, while he was in Europe, she was "bewitched, bothered and bewildered."

It was only when she finally arrived in Europe hoping to catch up with him (and successfully eluded by him) that the scales began to drop from her eyes. To describe her love affair in terms of Tin Pan Alley is not to trivialize it. She herself trivialized it by descending to sophomoric levels of self-abasement in her adoration of her tin god.

Yet it is this extraordinary affair of the heart and soul that is perhaps most revealing of her, and of her emotional needs.

9

I do not really want to get deeply involved with James Apthorp. As I have said, I've already had several unfortunate experiences with Harvard men. But we do seem to match in temperature. Both, at least now, at the beginning, very cool. Like Margaret with Emerson, I want to engage his intellect. In the 1990s educated women don't expect to be treated like bimbos. We might be open to an affair, but it would have to be an *intelligent* affair.

I find it important to establish that James and I match not only in temperature, but in intellect. After all, we are colleagues, on similar tenure tracks at our respective institutions. You might say we are inching along those tracks at roughly the same rate, and that, that inching—that bumpy progression, if you will—gives us a common goal and destiny. Thus, our dinners together after a day at the

Houghton, at one or another of the Harvard Square hang-outs, are characterized by serious discussions of American literature or culture, or the latest exhibition at the Museum of Fine Arts, or the most recent international crisis in Washington. Such discussions also ring with a certain amount of argumentative one-upmanship, as if we are competing not only as scholars, but for a job as critic or correspondent for *The Boston Globe* or *The New York Times*. At such times, I notice James's blue eyes darken. I attribute this to the intensity with which he pursues his thoughts. Often, however, we circle quickly back to our favorite topics: Margaret and Melville.

Margaret and Melville are our M & M's, more tasty to our ravenous intellectual tongues than any chocolate could ever be. Chocolate, after all, is said to signify love, and our literary M & M's provide, I feel, the appropriate romantic mood. Our discussions can on some levels be counted as working sessions on our respective books. I have already sampled a small bit of adhesive feeling in my short encounters with Natasha Owens. Now James's awareness of Melville's passion for Hawthorne might further extend my understanding of Margaret's adhesiveness. I emerge from these meals mentally stimulated and anxious to get back to my notes. Nothing physical has as yet passed between us, but that is the way we want it.

About a month into our friendship, James says:

—I've been working with Melville's European journal. He called Lucrezia Borgia a "good looking dame."

—He never wrote that way for publication, did he? I've often wondered if the literary styles we deal with are very different from the way they spoke in the nineteenth century.

—Judging from his journal, he was quite colloquial when he was being casual. He also said The Louvre "beats the British Museum."

I start in on a comparative consideration of the collections of the Louvre and the British Museum (the Louvre, after all, has the Mona Lisa, and even better, Leonardo's *Virgin, Child, and Saint Anne*, but the British Museum has the Elgin Marbles.) This launches first a debate over the history and definition of "The Masterpiece," then an argument over whether or not Lord Elgin should have taken the marbles away from Greece.

JAMES: He preserved them.

ANGELICA: He had no right.

JAMES: They would be crumbling now from all the car fumes. They're preserved in the Museum as they never would be if exposed to all the toxic air we all breathe. We'll crumble too, soon enough.

ANGELICA: They belong to Greek culture, to their ancient heritage. What if somebody came over here and took away the Statue of Liberty?

JAMES: Don't be idiotic.

ANGELICA: Don't call me an idiot!

JOHN (*We are in a slightly better restaurant than usual and the*

waiter has informed us that his name is John): Would you
like to see the dessert menu?
JAMES: I could use something sweet.

I suppose you could call it our first fight. Each of us ends
the evening feeling a bit offended. I, feeling I deserve an apol-
ogy and James irritated, I realize, that I argued with him. Was
that part of Margaret's dilemma? Part of woman's universal
dilemma?

10

James Nathan took Margaret from the very beginning by surprise. He was a *blue-eyed* Jew:

> I have long had a presentiment that I should meet—nearly—one of your race, who would show me how the sun of today shines upon the ancient Temple—but I did not expect so gentle and civilized an apparition, and with blue eyes!

He was also German. Thoroughly enamored, like any self-respecting Transcendentalist, of German culture, Margaret could now insert occasional bits of German (*"Mein Leibster, Das ist hart!"*) into the epistolary bullets with which she shortly beseiged him, conveyed by a "small messenger" or "our little page."

The earliest letters begin as odes to nature, filled with "blue skies," "inspiring breezes" and trees in bloom, and rapidly become metaphorical: "... my mind has been enfolded in your thought, as a branch with a flame."

In a month's time, late March, Margaret is in the throes of romantic love. At the very moment when she is courageously denouncng in the *Tribune* the conditions at the Women's Penitentiary—"The want of proper matrons, or any matrons, to take the care so necessary for the bodily or mental improvement or even decent condition of the seven hundred women assembled here is an offence that cries aloud"—she is writing to James Nathan: "I hear you with awe assert power over me and feel it to be true ... I feel deep confidence in my friend and know that he will lead me on in a spirit of holy love and that all I may learn of nature and the soul will be legitimate."

AWE. POWER OVER ME. HOLY LOVE. NATURE. SOUL.

James Nathan (in whose defense, it must be said, was only human) is for Margaret a Transcendental dream, a sublime force of nature, powerful enough to exact the surrender of her soul to HOLY LOVE. If Margaret is not, in this instance, a nineteenth-century version of a groupie gushing over a rock star, she is close to it. After her death, Emerson finds in her papers the almost wailing entry: "I need a full, godlike embrace from some sufficient love."

Mind surrenders to Feeling, to some idea of love she has long cherished and never found. It is *amativeness*, not *adhesiveness* now.

The letter (Letter IX in Nathan's publication of her most private thoughts), one of those she surely wanted him to burn, continues: "I wish, I long to be human, but divinely human . . . Let the soul invest every act of its abode with somewhat of its own lightness and subtlety. Are you my guardian to domesticate me in the body, and attach it more firmly to the earth?"

I am talking this out with James over dinner.

—Domesticate her in her body? What was she thinking?

—Sex. *(James says, looking at me a bit curiously.)*

—Sex?

—Don't be so thick. What else? She's asking for it.

—She's WHAT?

—Angelica, believe me, she's a frustrated old maid.

My Margaret. A frustrated old maid. I recall that after her death, Emerson, reading through her papers, had decided she was a hysterical virgin. Now James is talking the same male talk as Emerson. I can hardly bear it. James and I have developed such a lovely friendship. I have begun to have romantic feelings about him. I see him in my mind's eye sometimes while I am at my work, see us walking together along the Charles with the water shining luminously beside us, see us talking animatedly at all our post-Houghton dinners.

He has begun to see me home, to give me sweet quick kisses goodnight. Nothing much. No tight embraces. I have firmly established that we have an intellectual rapport. Do I now want him to domesticate me in my body? Am I beginning to desire him? Did Margaret desire James Nathan ? *Was* she a frustrated old maid? And what am I? Not an old maid.

I've already tried marriage. Not even a virgin, as she surely was then. But isn't old maid a state of mind? I look at James Apthorp and begin to wonder about our perfect intellectual relationship. Are Margaret's letters beginning to wear on me? But James Apthorp is not a German Jew. The only thing he has in common with James Nathan are his blue eyes.

This night, James does not give me a quick good night kiss. This night, as he is leaving me, he puts his arms around me and draws me to him. I can feel his whole body against me. It is a long kiss now, complete with tongue. His tongue explores my mouth. His hand moves slowly onto my breast. My body starts to respond to his touch. My tongue starts a little dance with his tongue. Our tongues seem to have established some sort of complicity. I will not call it a communion. They are in harmony. Are we developing not only an intellectual harmony but a tongue harmony? Does tongue harmony portend a domestication of my body? I can see in his eyes when the kiss ends that something has begun to change between us. It is not long before tongue harmony turns into full physical harmony. It is not long before the one evening when he comes up into my bed.

11

As a German, James Nathan must have been susceptible to all Margaret's talk of soul and spirit. As you know, Margaret knew her Goethe by heart, had translated his conversations with Eckermann, had interested herself in the adhesive relationship of Bettina and Günderode, was familiar with Schiller and other German Idealists. But possibly what struck him most forcibly in Letter IX was the question: "Are you my guardian to domesticate me in the body...?"

Letter IX was written on a Sunday. By Tuesday (Letter X), the unspeakable had occurred. Margaret writes:

> Yesterday was, perhaps, a sadder day than I had in all my life. It did not seem to me an act of "Providence," but of some ill demon, that had exposed me to what was to every worthy and womanly feeling so humiliating.

Neither could I reconcile myself to your having such thoughts, and just when you had induced me to trust you so absolutely.

He had made a pass. How much of a pass is anyone's guess. Margaret had decided he was her soul's companion. Her body, still undomesticated, wanted little else but to float in the ether with him, perhaps to reach out and eat Emerson's metaphorical apple, and in eating it, eat the world. But worldly sensuality, she made very clear, was not what she had in mind: "You have said there is in yourself both a lower and a higher than I was aware of. Since you said this, I suppose I have seen that lower! It is—is it not? the man of the world, as you said you see 'the dame' in me. Yet shall we not both rise above it?"

In the same letter, she begs him to offer her:

[if not all] the truth, always, at least, tell me absolute truth . . . Wilt thou not come with me before God and promise me severe truth, and patient tenderness, that will never, if it can be avoided, misinterpret the impulses of my soul . . . Will an unfailing reverent love shelter the "sister of your soul?"

In "The Great Lawsuit" she had written: "A sister is the fairest ideal and how nobly Wordsworth, and even Byron, have written of a sister." Ah Margaret, Margaret, were you really so naive? Two poets with incestuous relationships with their sisters, and you totally blind to them? Byron, who did not share your admiration for de Staël, whom he found "nothing but a plain woman, forcing one to listen, and look at her, with her pen behind her ear, and her mouth full of ink." Byron, who was so madly in love with his sister Augusta, he could write: "What a fool I was to marry—and you not very wise—my dear—we might have lived so single and happy—as old maids and bachelors; I shall never find any one like you—nor you (vain as it may seem) like me. We are just formed to pass our lives together. . . . "

And Wordsworth, Wordsworth who subjected his wife to lifelong torment because he could not give up his incestuous love for his sister Dorothy, who became ill at the very thought of his wedding and then CAME TO LIVE WITH THEM.

And Margaret, Margaret, *you want to be the sister of James Nathan's soul?*

12

My own relationship with James Apthorp has been developing as I hoped it would. It is grounded in our mental rapport. We are colleagues, in the library and in our post-library discussions. We continue to consume our intellectual M & M's. He is currently immersed in the Melville-Hawthorne saga, so filled with desire on Melville's part, so warily rejected on Hawthorne's. I am pondering the implications of the James Nathan romance, surely the most devastating love relationship of Margaret's life, the one where her whole sense of her own womanliness is challenged.

James and I now have a physical rapport as well. Our bodies have established the mutual comfort suggested by that initial tongue dance. James is a considerate lover, perhaps more passionate than I. But he accepts whatever limits on our activities I impose. I do impose some, of course. I don't like things to get sweaty or messy. I'm not too happy about body fluids. I love, when it is over, to continue to talk about Margaret and Melville, though he prefers to fall asleep. He sleeps for a while and then leaves. It is never an overnight thing. I don't mind. I like to get up alone and work on Margaret.

Soon, a portion of my Margaret work will be published in a small literary magazine. I am delighted. It will be my first time in print. I must admit to being a bit disappointed in James's reaction.

—Published where?

—*New England Ruminations.*

—Never heard of them.

—They deal with New England history and culture. I'll be in the spring issue, along with a piece on Anne Hutchinson and one on Lidian Emerson.

James fiddles with his food at another of our post-Houghton meals, picking up a stalk of broccoli and pushing it to the side of his plate with marked distaste for anti-oxidants. Finally, he says:

—Who cares about *Lidian* Emerson?

—They're not strictly a feminist magazine but they focus a lot on women's issues. *(I am eating my broccoli like a good little girl.)*

—What do they pay?

—I have no idea. I'll be in print.

His eyes have turned black.

—Women's stuff *(he snorts)*. You're wasting your time.

I am beginning to worry about James. My own work seems

to be progressing faster. Though neither of us is fully secure, his future seems less so. He has political problems in his department. Now they're not even sure they can get him tenure. It seems it was only a "hopeful" tenure track he was on, not a real one. He's in danger of being cast out into the world of the so-called independent scholar. No steady check. No security. Adjunct jobs that are part of the exploitativeness of the academic system. Maybe his reaction to my article is just nerves. Thoroughly understandable under the circumstances.

13

James Nathan seems to have continued the relationship on Margaret's terms, allowing her to be the kind of "sister" she wanted to be. Gifting her with a white veil. A WHITE VEIL! To celebrate her nunlike status? To reassure her that he respected the purity of their love? Evidently she did not mind erotic kisses and caresses in her adhesive relationships, but a fully amative relationship draws a different response from her.

Clearly, her pious invocations are more than any man can bear, much less a man like James Nathan, who all this time has been living with a young English mistress, passed off to Margaret as a homeless waif to whom he has given shelter. When Margaret discovers the girl's existence, she is totally taken in: "Could the heart of woman refuse its sympathy to this earnestness in behalf of an injured woman?" She is searching for truth. She cannot or will not penetrate the lies. Does she deceive herself about his feelings and intentions throughout their relationship? Her self-deception in this instance flies in the face of her indomitable, indeed, incomparable intellect.

What was going on? How many women who have closed their eyes to romantic betrayal have followed upon Margaret in the century and a half since her death?

He leaves his guitar with her. Then his dog, a Newfoundland puppy named Josey. She allows her dream of their love to envelop her, especially to revive feelings of childhood: "I should have been happy to be thus led by the hand through green and sunny paths, or like a child to creep close to the side of my companion, listening long to his stories of things, unfamiliar to my thoughts."

Yet her childhood had been miserable! Timothy Fuller had exacted a terrible price from the daughter who should have been a son, whom he educated as though she were a boy. The child who had blood dreams because of the *Aeneid* never had a real childhood. Though she might not have become the formidable Margaret Fuller without that early education, did one part of her want to be a bimbo, however holy? "I am with you as never with any other one. I like to be quite still and have you the actor and the voice. You have life enough for both; you will indulge me in this dear repose."

Margaret! The internationally recognized conversationalist whom Emerson will recommend to Carlyle for her wit. Margaret is, with James Nathan, WITHOUT VOICE.

Something else happens. By letter XIX on April 15th:

What passed yesterday, seemed not less sad today. The last three days have effected as violent a change as the famous three days of Paris, and the sweet little garden, with which my mind had surrounded your image, lies all desecrated and trampled by the hoofs of the demon who conducted this revolution, pelting with his cruel hailstones me, poor child, just as I had laid aside the protections of reserve, and laid open my soul in a heavenly trust. . . .

She knows now that he will leave: "I received, indeed with surprise, the intelligence that you would go away. It startled me for the moment with a sense, that you did not prize me enough."

Clearly he has found it necessary to exit as soon as possible. How to extricate himself from a situation in which Margaret is demanding such purified perfection?

She then chastises him as she has all the objects of her affections with a refrain by now fully familiar to us: "I had felt that I could be so much to you to refine, expand and exalt."

He has, in those mysterious three days, tried to make clear to her that he could never be to her what she wants. She wants his heart "and you have cruelly hung it up quite out of my reach, and declare: I shall never have it. *Oh das ist hart*! For no price! There is something I am not to have at any price. *Das ist hart*. You must not give it away in my sight at any rate. . . . "

Though she sounds resigned to the fact that he does not love her as she does him, she says, "My guardian angel must take better care of me another time and make me still more timid, for truly nothing but perfect love will give a man patience to understand a woman, even such a man as you, who have so much of feminine sweetness and sensibility."

If only she were more timid, he might love her. She must squelch even further the formidable Margaret, squelch what has been described by Emerson as her "mountainous Me." She must curb her natural instincts to assert herself. She must be what most men expect of woman, then and now. And he would balance what is left of her "masculine imprint" with his own androgyny, his "feminine sweetness and sensibility."

14

By Letter XX, Margaret has taken all the blame on herself:

> It is then, indeed myself who have caused all ill. It is I, who by flattering myself and letting others flatter me that I must ever act nobly and nobler than others, have forgot that pure humility which is our only safeguard. I have let self-love, pride and distrust creep upon me and mingle with my life-blood.

She abases herself: "I will now kneel, and, laying thy dear hand upon my heart, implore that if pride or suspicion should hide there again, the recollection of this day may rise up, and with its sharp deep pulse, make them flutter their wings. . . . "

She will then drive them out.

Now comes a startling revelation: "I have indeed always had a suspicion that I was not really good at all. . . . "

Margaret. Arrogant, self-assured Margaret. Is this true?
Has he succeeded in filling her with self-doubt? I find these
letters increasingly hard to bear. What is he doing to her
sense of herself, her noble self, her able self? She admits to
an alienation from self hardly ever expressed in her life and
actions. She humbles herself. *Oh God! She will not let go!* He is
hard put to escape her.

Finally, after several more letters in which she bemoans
the moonlight without him, gathers flowers for him ("I gathered two buds, one for you and one for me"), speaks of a
spirit passing through her that "ought to flow to you like
blessing . . . the most beautiful feeling I ever experienced; it
is indeed divine, and too much for mortal force . . . " and
refers to times of "pure soul communion . . . almost too
much for my strength," he has clearly had enough. Her letters beseech: "You come not, dear friend. The day was full of
golden sunlight, and kind words and deeds as well, for the
thought of you stood at the end, but you come not."

Margaret is now falling ill. She has always been prone to terrible headaches and insomnia. But now, by Letter XXVII:
". . . last night the pain in my neck became so violent, that I
could not lie still and passed a night suffering and sleepless."
In subsequent letters, she yearns to be a child again:
"Perhaps it is, that I was not enough a child at the right time,
and am now too childish; but will you not have patience
with that?" She feels powerless: ". . . often I feel, that you are
thinking of me and it takes away all power of thought or
motion." She quotes Novalis: "No angel can ascend to

heaven / Till the whole heart has fallen to the earth in ashes." She sends him one of her own poems, "To the Face Seen in the Moon", which includes the lines, "I am the mother of thy spirit life, / And so in law thy wife; / And thou art my sire."

After he leaves for London she writes: ". . . the effect of our intercourse was to make me so passive; sometimes I wonder it was so interesting to you, and yet I do not, for I seem a part of yourself." She reveals unsuspectingly how he tried to extricate himself with that most familiar of male excuses: "Once you intimated that you should not want a real correspondence with me while on your pilgrimage, for you needed to be 'unaccompanied' and quite free to receive new impressions. I thought this very natural and acquiesced."

How many wives before and since have heard that refrain? "Unaccompanied and quite free?" Women who have borne children, and slaved away—yes slaved—at housework, even with modern conveniences, have taken the brunt, the very brunt of domesticity, which drains the day with every conceivable small interruption, from grocery shopping to mice in the basement, who have been stalwart for their children and husbands in the face of every disaster, large and small, from minor illnesses and accidents to bankruptcy and heart attacks, from small humiliations at school to public shame, only to hear finally, when their husbands start turning gray and a bit paunchy: "I need to be unaccompanied and quite free to receive new impressions." In our society, it is known as a midlife crisis, and usually implies another woman on the scene or soon to arrive there.

Margaret was not married to James Nathan, but the principle was the same. Further, she was drowning him in principle, noble principle, and the other woman was there, had always been there, in the guise of the homeless waif. Even after he has finally gone, definitively left, returned to those European shores she has not yet experienced, to write some dispatches from Europe for the *Tribune* (an opportunity she has secured for him by intervening with Greeley), she writes: "I think with the utmost pathos of your poor maiden returning to her parents ... I shall always regret that I did not in some way see her so as to have in my mind her image. . . . " Indeed.

We shall never know what she looked like, that woman who filled James Nathan's sensual needs in ways unknown and mysterious to Margaret. We do not have in our minds her image. But we can see Margaret, perhaps quite plain, trying to rely on intellect and morality in the face of what may or may not have been superior attraction. Perhaps the other woman in this case was simply willing.

My relation to my own James is also becoming difficult. Tonight when we leave the library he excuses himself to run ahead, saying he has an appointment. The "appointment" greets him at the corner. I see them as I turn in that direction. I am stunned.

She is wearing high-heeled sandals, what some people have referred to as "fuck-me shoes." She has on a very tiny miniskirt and a tight blouse. With her long blond hair she looks like someone out of "Baywatch." I've seen such women on the covers of the *National Enquirer* at the supermarket. There will be no M & M's for James tonight. I am upset and agitated that he will not be with me either, that we will not be making love in my studio. We have never gone to his place. Does the "appointment" go to his place? Does she perhaps inhabit it? Who is she to him? I have found myself more and more looking forward to making love with James, though it has not been a very abandoned act. Could I be more abandoned? Let more body juices flow?

I look down at my midcalf skirt and running shoes, so easy for tramping across campus. Should I change my shoes? Bleach my hair? Let it grow from its short practical cut? Perhaps, like Margaret, I should just still my voice. Now that I see James with another woman, I am more aware of what he means to me. Are these feelings of amativeness? Of love? What has love done to Margaret? To me? What indeed is love?

15

I am researching love. Like Margaret, I have an inordinate desire for knowledge. When I have thoroughly researched love, I will understand it better, understand all of them: Margaret, Emerson, James Nathan, even James Apthorp and Natasha Owens. Will I understand myself? I hope so. My own self has experienced a partial surrender since I have been inhabited by the Margaret-Ghost.

More and more, I feel her moving inside me, inside my intellect, but also inside my woman's body. How universal are her feelings? How freely can they be transposed from one century to another, from one woman to another? From one *intelligent* woman to another. I don't like to be prideful, about either my intelligence or Margaret's, but it is intellect that binds me to her, and intellect in women has long threatened their relations with men.

Is there a distinction to be made between the intelligent woman and the intellectual one? Is general intelligence more tolerated by the male of the species? Is it the intellectual aspect, the erudition, the knowledge of books, of words, of ideas, of music, of art, that men reject?

Margaret was erudite. There is no doubt of that. Her father had seen to it. Had seen to it that she knew her *Aeneid*, regardless of the blood dreams and nightmares. How much his son did he make her? How much his son did she want to be?

My research on love has been voluminous. There is really no end to it. When I attack it through psychology, I stumble over Freud, to whom I have never felt as friendly as Jung. Freud himself was not so friendly to women. How could he be, when he wrote: "Throughout the ages, the problem of woman has puzzled people of every kind; you too will have pondered over this question in so far as you are men. From the women among you that is not to be expected, for you are the riddle yourselves."

So, Freud does not expect women to penetrate their own mystery. Freud is all about penis envy. Is that what Margaret had? Did she really want her tiny clitoris to elongate like Pinocchio's nose and become a penis, an organ of penetration? That is how women of intellect are often seen, as women who have opted out of their sexual role and place, who want to be other than they are. Margaret had even said of intellect that there "in sight at least I am a man."

The Freudians see women as passive orifices, beset by penis envy and masochistically afflicted. Was Margaret torn by such feelings? Did all her glorious intellect, her magnificent MIND boil down to penis envy? Add to this all the ramifications of the so-called Electra/Oedipus Complex. The transfer from her mother's garden to her role as her father's mate and lover. She would have done anything to please him. To become his daughter/son. To maintain the bisexuality that psychologists tell us is the norm for the developing child, so that in at least some instances, she was a man. Does this account for her love affairs with Caroline Sturgis and Anna Barker? Was this simply, in psychoanalytic terms, a retention of prepubertal bisexuality?

But why not put it more simply? Margaret wanted to *be* loved. She didn't care which sex loved her, as long as her love was returned. The return of love, the *being* the love object, this was her real goal.

And if she had to sacrifice intellect to do so, so be it. She had prized intellect all her life. Above all else. But is it possible that intellect became for her, with James Nathan, a flaw she had to relinquish in order to achieve her real goal? How else explain her mindless annexation of the non-voice, of ultimate passivity? Yet all this had to be conducted above the level of the flesh, for Margaret was not then, not yet, a European. Margaret was an American, born of puritan stock, with a long history of puritan values behind her, with Salem ancestors somewhere far in the background, capable of the Boston marriages which were, nominally at least, "above the flesh" even if she did sleep on Sam's pillow with Anna Barker when Sam was away, but incapable of accepting James Nathan's advances, for that is surely what happened.

As she had indicated to Emerson, she wanted Celestial Love. James Nathan, as a German, should have been capable of that, for in the nineteenth century, where else but in Germany did one find so much Celestiality?

Only in America. Only American Transcendentalism could equal the heights of celestial bonding broached by the German Idealists. But then, of course, James Nathan was a German Jew, and perhaps subscribed more fully to the idea of procreation of life in the here and now that had enabled his people to survive thousands of years of prejudice and exile. And procreation was of the flesh. As clearly James Nathan wanted Margaret to be.

So here was the real problem. James Nathan was of the flesh. Margaret wanted him to be of the spirit. Wanted their spirits to coincide, a heaven on earth in her fantasy of romantic love. And more, even more. Though she was willing to relinquish her intellect, to be awed and without voice, to be the vessel into which he could pour all his desires; it was a chaste vessel, a pure one, disinfected of earthly desire, though ultimately ultrafeminine in its passivity.

A chaste Stepford Wife! Margaret Fuller! Surely one of the greatest female intellects of the American nineteenth century. I reel at the thought of it.

Yet it is clear from her letters to James Nathan that Margaret was willing to be a Barbie Doll for him. From bringing her intellect and erudition to a peak of fulfillment, one hardly attained by any woman, anywhere, any time—and at a time when she was writing articles for Greeley's *Tribune* that dealt not only with the women in the penitentiary at Blackwell's Island, but the plight of prostitutes, and the tragic creatures in Bloomingdale's Asylum for the Insane—Margaret, who defended the Irish immigrants against prejudice and intolerance, admiring their "truth to domestic ties, their powers of generous bounty, and more generous gratitude, their indefatigable good-humour (for ages of wrong which have driven them to so many acts of desperation, could never sour their blood at its source) their ready wit, their elasticity of nature," Margaret was wishing for a guardian angel to "make me more timid."

She was writing to James Nathan that she would kneel before him.

KNEEL? This is the woman who wrote in *Woman in the Nineteenth Century* that ". . . it is a vulgar error that love, a love, to woman is her whole existence; she also is born for Truth and Love in their universal energy."

It was Margaret herself who wrote in that same extraordinary manifesto: "I have urged on woman independence of man, not that I do not think the sexes mutually needed by one another, but because in woman this fact has led to an excessive devotion, which has cooled love, degraded marriage, and prevented either sex from being what it should be to itself or the other."

Margaret, who wanted to incite women to exert their moral power in the cause of abolition, who published pieces against slavery from her *Tribune* pulpit, who found in women a magnetic element far more prevalent than in men, who saw women of genius as "overladen with electricity," frightening those around them. Women like the actress Rachel, whose morals upset even the tolerant French. Margaret, who herself had such powerful currents of electricity running through her that Emerson spoke of having to "stand from under." Margaret, who so upset Emerson by her magnetic presence that he had to use his small son as messenger between them when she visited his Concord home, driving Lidian mad with jealousy, because it was bad enough to live with the ghost of Ellen Tucker, who had died too soon after marrying Emerson—died while she was still young and beautiful, her lips stained with consumptive blood, so that he could mourn her forever—and found only in Margaret a woman who could, if she could not claim his romantic love, at least absorb his thoughts and entertain his intellect. Yet for poor Lidian he had neither romantic love nor intellectual feeling.

For Margaret, however, the coolness was too much. "I was greatly disappointed in my relation to him," she wrote, "... we do not act powerfully on one another." When she left Concord, she left on the old Margaret refrain: "... we do not fully meet, and to me you are too much and too little by turns." After she died, John Jay Chapman thought there was something pathetic, even cruel, in Emerson's incapacity to deal with her: "This brilliant woman was asking for bread and he was giving her a stone. ..."

The stone was too hard. The temperature too cool.

And when James Nathan came along, the brilliant author of *Woman in the Nineteenth Century* begged for bread. In the same year that she published those words, Truth and Love in the universal sense were abandoned. She was justifying the "vulgar error" that love to woman was her whole existence. But also in that year—such were the ruptures that consumed her—in writing about prison and asylum reform, she quotes this bit of prose poetry: "The Mind is the intellectual part of the soul. It is spiritual . . . It is invisible. It is intangible. It is without color . . . It is without weight. It is supposed to be situated in the head. It dwells in the brain, on whose throne it sits . . . It is the most important and noblest part of our system."

What happened to Margaret's noble mind in James Nathan's presence? How much was she willing to subdue its ability to "think, conceive, imagine, reflect, remember, recognize or recollect . . . ?" Had she literally lost her mind over this man? Does it make any sense to demand equality for women in the abstract, then retract the demand when "the right man" appears? And who is the right man? The one who makes you kneel? Surrender your mind? Humble yourself? Pretend to be a bimbo?

Scratch any intelligent woman, even at the end of the enlightened twentieth century, and she will nod her head in assent. A right man had come along (one could, of course, argue that there are several possible rights, if she is lucky) but he had not liked Mind. Mind was invisible, intangible, without color or weight, but it was still Mind, and it was situated in woman's brain, where for the most part, men preferred it not to be.

But then why did James Nathan dally with Margaret at all? Is it conceivable that he tolerated her brain, which housed, presumably, her mind, but was bothered even more

by her morals, her excess of "nobility," her outrage at whatever pass or passes he had made? He was willing to talk
about Celestial Love, something she had discussed at length
with Emerson, for a reasonable amount of time, but then,
but then, there was not only a soul, inhabited by mind, or
inhabiting mind, as the case might be, there was also a body.
Body and Soul. As the song goes: *"Are you pretending, it looks
like the ending, unless I can have one more chance to prove, dear?"*
When James Nathan said it was the ending, he must have
known it from the beginning. Otherwise, why the homeless
waif for whom Margaret showed such innocent, unsuspect-
ing sympathy?

James Apthorp breaks into my thoughts. What do I do about
James Apthorp? Is he a very different kind of James? After
all, he shares Margaret's puritan background. But if he
shares that background, surely he also cares about Mind. He
must be the exception. He must be a rare right kind of man.
He is, after all, a Harvard intellectual. Surely he appreciates
Mind in woman. All our M & M conversations attest to it. I
haven't rejected his passes, or placed too much emphasis on
morality. I haven't upset him, as Margaret did *her* James. I
am, after all, sleeping with him, though admittedly, our
times together are growing fewer and fewer. He seems to
have more and more appointments after our time in the
library. I have not seen him again with the Baywatch girl,
but I suspect that she is there, somewhere. I am trying hard
to be less reserved in bed, to allow more juices to flow. But I
find it hard. As Margaret said, *"Das ist hart."*

It is difficult too to wear more Baywatch-y clothing. I tried buying a pair of fuck-me shoes, but my feet hurt. It is very difficult to wear them in Cambridge with all the cobblestones. It takes forever to cross Harvard Yard. No, the shoes were not a good idea. But neither was the short skirt, which continually made me feel that someone could look up my dress. I spent half my time in Houghton tugging my skirt down. And the cleavage bra from Victoria's Secret made me self-conscious. Actually, it's a most interesting concept. You can cantilever in four positions, I kid you not. Four positions! High, higher, higher, higher still. The higher still, of course, gives the most cleavage. But even the least high is rather impressive. But looking at myself in the mirror, I don't feel like myself. It's like writing a popular novel: either you have the head for it or you don't. If you don't, you can't fake it, can't make a million from a blockbuster bestseller. Editors and readers can always tell. I don't have the head for it. I'll stick to my study of Margaret. But neither do I have the head for seductive shoes and uplift bras. No. James Apthorp must like me for who I am. Surely our meeting of the minds, and our comfortable bed-sharing count for something.

Yet, I find it is all making me a bit uneasy. James and I continue to have our M & M conversations. He has been delving even deeper into Melville's relation to Hawthorne, which is especially interesting to me, since Hawthorne was so disagreeable about Margaret. Not only did he turn her (despite Henry James's doubts) into Zenobia; in *The Blithedale Romance*, he wrote after her death: "She had a strong and coarse nature, which she had done her utmost to refine, with infinite pains, but of course it could only be superficially changed . . . she proved herself a very woman after all, and fell as the weakest of her sisters might."

Margaret! In Hawthorne's eyes, and I do believe in his eyes alone, "strong and coarse." And what are we to think of the "very woman" bit? By this, he has to have meant her marriage/non-marriage to Ossoli.

Ossoli is another issue, one I will deal with later on. But *coarse* is a strange word to use in relation to Margaret. Of course, it seems questionable if Margaret was ever Hawthorne's kind of woman. I suspect he did not like strong women, or strongly intellectual ones. I suspect he was suspicious of Mind in woman. And he was certainly suspicious of male affection for men. Melville's adoration made Hawthorne very nervous indeed.

James has been a bit reluctant to talk about same-sex love. Yet we have both had to deal with the problem in our shared M & M's. James doesn't want to emphasize the adhesive aspect of Melville. He'd rather think of him as an adventurer, an intellectual pirate on the high seas, leaving behind Fayaway with a putative son, according to subsequent visitors to the South Seas. James seems to share a certain general macho discomfort with bisexuality. In fact, there are times when James surprises me with his degree of machismo. It seems to surface especially when I have just given a guest lecture on Margaret. There is applause and appreciation, but when I look at James, he seems to be scowling and upset. He always tells me it was fine, but he always treats me more brusquely, and never comes to my bed afterwards. I am still trying to figure this out.

Meanwhile my work is going well. More and more, I am asked to lecture about Margaret, or about Margaret and Emerson. I find these talks very satisfying. Sometimes they are at Harvard colloquia, sometimes at my college, and sometimes outside academia, to interested groups, women's groups who are fixated on Margaret as a feminist pioneer. On these occasions, I don't talk too much about the James Nathan business, because what am I to say? That Margaret in love humbled herself? That she would have submitted to the worst form of male domination? That she would have sacrificed her soul, *her soul being her mind*, for James Nathan's love?

I'm telling it true in my written text—somehow it is easier to confide it to the page—but I can't yet speak it aloud. It feels blasphemous.

I have stopped inviting James to these events because he seems so grumpy afterwards. He has been having a somewhat rougher time of it. His article on Melville was refused by the New England Society for Melville Studies. A new book on Melville has just surfaced, preempting some of his ideas. And to top it all off, he's gotten swamped in a consideration of Melville as a depressive. I agree. He was.

—But James, I say, as we are walking home one moonlit night from Houghton, with the moon in the Cambridge sky looking as it did when Allston painted it, and I am half thinking of Margaret looking at Allston's moons when she writes her famous criticism of the showing of his paintings in l839 at Chester Harding's studio.

—James, I say, why can't you admit that at least some of the depression came from Melville's sexual ambiguity? From his adhesive feelings for Hawthorne, which were, after all, rejected because Hawthorne couldn't, wouldn't, or didn't feel the same way? Besides that, Melville felt oppressed, surrounded by all the women in his family. His mother was so bossy and domineering. And his wife, Lizzie, made it all worse by humiliating him writing to everyone she knew, begging for a "job for Herman." And then he finally ended up in the Customs House. The greatest American writer of the nineteenth-century. Seen mainly as a writer of books about cannibals. Hardly recognized as still alive all the years he worked in the Customs House.

—His depression, James answers, like many great artists, stemmed from his lack of recognition. Hawthorne had nothing to do with it.

—But, I argue, not willing to let go of my point, I think his depression about Hawthorne, who was after all his great love, was as important as his critical rejection. You're dipping into psycho-biography without allowing the psychological factors to be properly weighed. You're hardly willing to read Freud.

—Dr. Fraud had a dick instead of a tongue.

—I admit Freud is too sexually fixated to be always useful. But I've used him with Margaret when it felt right.

James ends the conversation by glowering at me silently. He has taken to aborting our dialogues, to retreating into long silences. He is foundering because he cannot deal with Melville's adhesiveness. His macho is threatened by it. I'm beginning to think his macho is threatened by me, as well. We argue more and go to bed less. I've stopped wearing the hurtful fuck-me shoes. But I've let my hair grow longer and darkened my lipstick. And I've bought a Victoria's Secret bra, a more sedate, less highly cantilevered one. These cosmetic changes however do not seem to have helped. Indeed James seems not to have noticed them, to be oblivious to them. Rather, he seems to enjoy challenging my ideas with a surly face. I am torn between asserting my ideas and staying quiet. When I stay still, he seems content.

Is there something geisha-like in me at these moments? Does James, with his puritan background, and no Japanese blood or experience that I know of, want a geisha? Did James Nathan also want a geisha? Was Margaret willing to become one for him? But it was Margaret who protested against the idea that a noble, accomplished woman could be said to have "surpassed her sex." It was Margaret who proclaimed: "We would have every path laid open to woman as freely as to man."

Before, James was supportive of my work with Margaret. Now, he puts her down.

—She was a man in a woman's skirt.

—Why? Because she was intelligent? Is that a male prerogative, to be intelligent? Is it closed to women?

—A woman should be a woman. She had a man's head.

—She hated that. To be accused of having a "masculine

mind." Even though she sometimes liked the idea of feeling like a man in thought, at least.

—She *was* a man (James says glumly). She was a bloody boring guy! Why don't you write about a REAL woman?

—She *was* a real woman, in the fullest sense of the word.

—She was a les. All you feminists are leses.

—Are you calling me a LESBIAN?

—You make love like a les.

—How would *you* know, James? How many lesbians have *you* bedded?

He leaves to go home. No bed again.

The next evening, after the library, I watch him meet the Baywatch girl again. I am beginning to get the message. I am jealous, disturbed, agitated, in fact. *Was* I making love like a lesbian? How do lesbians make love? Are they more tender? More loving? Or are they more male than other women when in bed with a man? Do lesbians go to bed with men? Certainly bisexuals do.

Had James bedded, if not a lesbian, at least a bisexual? How do I research lesbians? Bisexuals?

Tomorrow, I must attend another departmental meeting. Natasha Owens could be my golden opportunity.

16

Sitting in the neutral, neutered space of the faculty meeting room, I survey them all again. These are the people who will determine my life's direction. If my work on Margaret pleases them, and after that, some other college committee, I will be tenured. TENURE is the cherished dream of everyone voyaging into academia. It is Shangri-La, even without Ronald Colman. With tenure comes the security not only of status and reputation, but of a TIAA-CREF pension. I could look forward not only to a substantial salary that no one can take away from me, but to a substantial retirement, when, since I don't play golf, I could travel.

Of course, at my reasonably young age (my early thirties) it is a bit hard to plan for my old age. But that's the whole point of tenure. I won't have to worry about any of that. To be tenured is to be free of having to look for a job, of having to worry about a check coming in. The checks always come in! Total security!

So getting tenure is like latching onto the best Life Security System. Provided you don't die of something else before you grow old (various diseases, plane crashes and so forth), you can grow old without fear of leaving Shangri-La, without fear, virtually, of the wrinkles showing. With tenure too, you are always young inside, because of the students. You keep up with the latest generation. You never fall behind.

John Denton, Margaretta Sinclair, Bill Lipton, and Natasha Owens are all present and accounted for. I am the only untenured faculty member here. The only one who is unsecured. Insecure? No, I am not really insecure. But unsecured, surely. I would like to be honest with them. I keep promising that my study of Margaret will soon be in their hands.

Will they hate my emphasis, my obsession, really, with love? With Margaret's loves and rejections? But wasn't that Margaret's center? Wasn't she really about love? Then what part did intellect play? We value her today not for her love-life, but for her intellect, for the woman who spoke out about woman's psyche, woman's soul, woman's essence and especially woman's mind. But also for the woman who could be a Transcendental philosopher, a brilliant journalist, an essayist, a poet, a champion of the African-American, the Indian, the prostitute on the street. All this is what has earned her her place in History.

Then why am I focusing on her loves? Her sad, unrequited loves? I must be mad, to risk my tenure on this focus. It is surely not politically correct of me. It is not what a feminist wants to hear. That Margaret wanted, ultimately, to be a bimbo. Do I want to be a bimbo? Is that what I think of when I think of competing with the Baywatch girl?

—Angelica, I hear John Denton asking, when can we expect to read a few chapters?

He is gesturing again with that ubiquitous pipe. He is looking at me with eyes that might even be reproachful.

—Very soon, John. I'm very close. Just tying up some loose bits of research.

—I don't mean to rush you, but the semester is moving on.

He is uttering a basic truth. Academic time flies. It is a flight that places it in a different realm than other time. Conditioned by the College Calendar, by midterm exams and papers due, by the relentless teleology of the syllabus, and by five-year curriculum planning by the administration, its unswerving trajectory heads towards welcome breaks (Christmas/Spring/Summer) that beckon so seductively one doesn't realize how time slips and slides away. Days are not days. Nights not nights. All is subject to the rule of the Calendar. And into that must be inserted, somehow, the research and writing that, in addition to teaching, qualifies for tenure. What about after tenure? Ah, yes. That depends on one's character. The true scholar will keep going. The rest will give up and sit on their security.

Which am I? I'm not sure I know. I always thought of myself as a scholar. But why am I so insistent on this business of Margaret's love? And what of the Baywatch girl? What of James Apthorp? What of the lesbian in bed?

I find myself studying Natasha Owens. She feels my eyes upon her and glances up and smiles. I sense no hard feelings about our last encounter.

When the meeting is over, I accept her invitation to another lunch, offered with a pseudo-apologetic air that does not deceive me. But here is my chance. Here is my invitation once again to understand Margaret's passion for other women. We go back to the apartment on Commonwealth Avenue, fronted so gracefully by trees, and screaming nineteenth-century Victorian. It is, as before, precise and neat. It is clear that Natasha has her belongings in order. What of her internal belongings? What of the inside of her head? What, for that matter, of the back of her head? Her amativeness, clearly defined by her straight black cut? How will I react if she makes another pass? Do I want her to? Do I secretly want her to?

She is bustling about the apartment. Getting out the plates, utensils, and placemats. Opening and closing the refrigerator from which emerge the makings of yet another salad. This time, she tells me, it will be a caesar. The south of France, the niçoise, had had no effect on me. But Caesar was after all a conqueror. Will I be her Brutus? Will I kill her, should she make an overture, with another rejection? James has begun to reject me. Margaret was so often rejected. Can

I bear to do that to another human being? But Natasha was hardly hurt by my first rebuff. This time, however, I feel could be different.

I help her in the preparation. I wash the lettuce, drying each leaf carefully with Bounty. There will be no *e. coli* bacteria in *my* lettuce. I break the egg, worrying about salmonella. We decide to half cook the egg. We are being very careful about diseases. Will we be as careful about other diseases, the maladies of the psyche? of gender? of love?

She is mixing in the croutons, which she has further browned in olive oil after they emerge from their Pepperidge Farm packaging.

—It isn't about sex, you know. Not really. I was half teasing you the other time.

—It didn't seem like teasing.

—I thought you would bolt like a scared rabbit. I just wanted to see if I was right

—If it's not about sex, then what?

She pops a crouton in her mouth and starts to add the grated parmesan, which she has just made fresh in the Cuisinart.

—It's about the whole damn male patriarchy. It's about making connection with those of us who are marginalized in this society. It's about feeling other than Other. Feeling solidarity with someone in the same boat by virtue of her gender, her chromosomes, things she can't help that she was born with, or without. To read Freud you would think we are all dying slowly because God cut off our penises. It's about refusing to be penalized for not having a penis. You notice that both words have the same root. Penis, penalized, penitentiary. It's about being caged because you're a woman. It's about self-love. About the Goddess.

—Margaret dealt a lot with the Goddesses in her "Conversations."

—She was trying to raise consciousness. To show those Boston women they could be proud of themselves, proud of their minds.

We are seated, now, and eating. Natasha's culinary skills are exemplary. She is no Martha Stewart, but it's a good salad, a sophisticated mix. But Martha Stewart, ostensibly a Stepford Wife, is really not that way at all. She's a great cook, and she can make a mean gingerbread house at Christmas time, infuriating all the working women who barely have time to shop for their kids, but she's also been the tough manager of a billion-dollar company, her towels and sheets running K-Mart.

What does that tell us? That Martha Stewart is a guerrilla fighter in the feminist trenches? That Martha Stewart only pretends to be brainless. That Martha Stewart has made a fortune out of feeding the patriarchal dream of *kinder, kirche, küche*. But her books sell in the millions. To WOMEN! Who have also bought into the patriarchal sell.

So what am I doing here with Natasha? Am I trying to discover something about Margaret and women? About her love for Anna Barker, who betrayed her by marrying Samuel Ward and turning him from Margaret's "Raffaello," her dream and his of an artistic career, into a *banker?* Is this also about Margaret's James, or is it about my James and the Baywatch girl?

—Women, Natasha is saying, want a whole relationship. Men just want sex. That's your problem.

—How do you mean, my problem?

—You want a whole relationship. With anyone, man or woman. I made a pass at you but you knew it was just sex. I just wanted to see what you'd do.

—And what if we had a whole relationship? I ask, thinking that I must tell her about getting a moisturizer for her wrinkles. Ivana Trump has said that if she were ship-wrecked on a desert island the one thing she must have would be her moisturizer. Can I have a whole relationship with Natasha if she doesn't know about moisturizers? What if it is just as I originally thought, a feminist anti-bias? Does she shave under her armpits? Surely not. But then, neither does Julia Roberts, whose smile can light up the world.

She has been eyeing me pensively, munching on a crouton.

—Let's try a whole relationship. Then we'll see . . .

—See what?

—Just see, she answers cryptically.

She makes no passes today. It is warm and comfortable in her apartment. I feel cozy and cossetted, and no longer on guard. We talk a bit more about Margaret. She hasn't read the James Nathan letters. When I tell her about them, she seems annoyed, almost outraged.

—She couldn't have been such an idiot.

—She was. I couldn't believe it myself.

—She fell into that whole damned patriarchal romance shit.

—I can't figure it out.

—You will. I'll help you. It's a deep well. You'll climb out of it.

I look at her doubtfully. My mind turns to James Apthorp and the Baywatch girl. I look down at my foot, visualizing beneath my sensible running shoe the bunion caused by the fuck-me shoes.

I hope she is right.

Back home, I find that I can't get back to work. Natasha has confused me, more now than when she made a pass. Was Margaret really right? Is same-sex love just as easy? Could it be easier? Not just the sex. The love. But is the love possible without the sex? Could I really stay in the stratosphere if I loved Natasha Owens? But how could I love Natasha Owens? I hardly know her. She's right about the whole relationship thing. I need a whole relationship. Would a whole relationship be easier with another woman? At least another woman is not Other. Not another gender. Not someone who might not understand what it feels like to be a woman, a member of the female gender. This gender business is getting to me, as I suppose it got to Margaret. As the song goes, *"I'm a WOMAN."*

And what, for God's sake, does that really mean?

That I have two x chromosomes. That x chromosomes, of which men have only one, are larger than the male y. Six times larger. And a y is simply an x without its extra leg. Because of my chromosomes, I have two breasts and no penis. But who would really want a penis? What woman would really want a penis? Freud is so wrong there. Compare. Just compare. The luscious, fruitlike breasts of a woman, like great juicy melons, with a male penis. Rather like a turkey neck. And even smaller, when not aroused, just a limp little appendage. An x without its extra part. And because of this, the whole patriarchal society has assumed dominance. Negating woman's role, her potential, her intellect, and concentrating, yes even fixating, like a Victoria's Secret catalogue, on woman's breasts.

Would Margaret have fared better if her breasts had equalled her vast intellect? She would never have needed implants, never have had to worry about the Baywatch girl or cantilevered bras. She would have had the vastest breasts on the North American continent. In France, it is true, she might have had to compete with Germaine de Staël, or even George Sand, who hid her breasts under her male clothes and pseudonym. Who hardly used the lovely name she had—Aurora. What patriarchal taboos made her exchange a name like Aurora, *Dawn of Day*, *Goddess of Dawn* (a Goddess, for Heaven's sake!) for a name like George?

She was George outside, maybe, in her male clothes like Marlene Dietrich, but inside she was Aurora, recognizeable at core by any other woman. True? Maybe. Maybe not. Maybe there are many kinds of women, many more than have been recognized. There is the Stepford Wife woman, the *kinder, kirche, küche* woman, upgraded to the Martha Stewart woman who has time to make gingerbread houses, and there is also, now especially, the woman who works, and the woman who uses her intellect.

In Margaret's day, Intellect was a male faculty. If women had Intellect, they were supposed to evict the gene from its place on the x chromosome. Take it off, like a bead on a string. Suppress it, if it was not removable. Women were allowed to make art, up to a point: dainty watercolors of flowers or fruit. Embroidery. Mourning pictures. Decapitators of male offenders, like Artemesia Gentileschi earlier, were hardly tolerated. Writers could be suspect. Actresses, even more so.

Yet women were recognized as creatures of intuition and feeling, and surely the arts required these attributes then as now, as always. With other women, at least, Margaret could have felt some understanding, some common ground of mutual recognition. This is surely what she found with Caroline Sturgis and Anna Barker. Could I find this with Natasha Owens? Should I try? Would I try, if only in the interests of my same-sex, adhesive research? Would a relationship with Natasha Owens alleviate my despair over the Baywatch girl? For I must admit, I am in despair over the Baywatch girl. Over James Apthorp and the Baywatch girl, and why he should prefer the Baywatch girl to me and to our M & M's.

I leave to go to the library. Maybe tonight James will come home with me. I am too filled with heterosexual romantic sentiment to give up hope that James and I will unite our xx and xy chromosomes in some lasting way that will match our M & M compatibility.

This night, for whatever reason, James does indeed seem willing to extend that compatibility to my bed. Perhaps my few cosmetic changes, my minor cantilevered concessions are having some effect. He is increasingly puzzled by the Hawthorne/ Melville relationship. It has obliged him to dig deeper into Hawthorne.

ANGELICA: It's strange how Melville was so macho on one hand, and so clearly bisexual on the other.

JAMES: Hawthorne was very threatened by him.

ANGELICA: I admire Melville for it. He didn't stand on false macho.

JAMES: Hawthorne *was* ambiguous about his own sexuality. He held onto it by putting his wife in her place.

ANGELICA: This *woman's place* business is something I could never understand.

JAMES: That's because you're a woman.

ANGELICA: And what does *that* mean? That women can't understand anything? That our intelligence is inferior?

We have just been making love. I am still lying with my naked leg thrust across his, leaning back on my pillow, as my breasts rise before me. My fruits,the results of my xx chromosomes. I have been feeling very feminine. Now, suddenly, I am feeling very feminIST. I feel him recoil. He moves his leg, gets up slowly, and starts to dress. His turkey neck has shrunk until it is hardly visible. I have had a bad effect on his turkey neck. With the Baywatch girl, it might have remained extended.

My intellect has forced this withdrawal, not only of his member, but of his affection. I must try harder not to insert it into our relationship. I must still myself in the future. I must not insert my mind and words into our bed. Otherwise, the day will come when he hesitates to insert himself into me. And if the physical joining goes, as even Hawthorne knew, and intimated about his own marriage, much of the love feeling goes as well. James has, of course, never said he loves me. But he must, mustn't he? I have so much to offer him.

17

I have begun the Ossoli folder. It is yellow for the Italian sun. Ossoli brought two golden suns into Margaret's life: the Italian sun and her own son, Nino. Despite the war, despite all their tragic deaths, Ossoli gave Margaret two suns, one for each of her twin Gemini souls.

But the Ossoli mystery remains the greatest puzzle of all. How to account for the Ossoli relationship? She was not Katharine Hepburn, and he was not Rossano Brazzi. It was not even Venice. It was Rome, where, incidentally, if you walk about in the area around the Piazza Navona, you can still find the Ossoli Palace, suitably signed for tourists, but with no mention of Margaret. The family was titled, but probably not very well off. Marchese Giovanni Angelo d' Ossoli looks (in the photo of him preserved in Houghton) with his moustache and high-tied cravat, like a dandy—or a superior organ-grinder. Perhaps a bit of both. His eyes are dark and intense, his gaze direct, his stance erect, perhaps predetermined by the requirements of portrait photography at the time. Whether or not he was clamped still, like so many early daguerreotype subjects, is hard to determine. I can picture him as the Italian suitor in a Merchant-Ivory film, and indeed Margaret, when she lived on the Via del Corso on the second floor of number 514, had a room with a view. Looking down at the crowds, at the panorama of busyness, one can sense a connection with the life of the street that had long escaped her in New England.

He approached her in St. Peter's in Easter Week of 1847. She had lost her travelling companions, the Springs, in the vast cathedral. She herself was lost, or at least appeared so, as she wandered around the various chapels, savoring the art, the space, Michelangelo's dome, having passed first through Bernini's colonnade, and then, inside, confronted his extraordinary convoluted Baldacchino.

What could be more antithetical to puritan simplicity than baroque splendor, the wingedness of baroque space, a seventeenth-century anticipation of the relativity principle? She must have been enjoying that rarified Italian taste of the sublime in a masterpiece of architecture, in culture, which was, in Italy, as Henry James later put it, "out in the streets," while in America sublimity was more readily to be found in nature's handiwork. But she must also have been pleased that the young man, roughly ten years younger (27 to her 37, long before it was fashionable for the woman to have this chronological primacy) had noticed her, wanted to serve as her guide.

Let us forget for a moment the demonstrated fact that Italian men will notice any female of whatever age—I have seen them pinch aged grandmothers. Let us rather take it from the romantic viewpoint. There was an attraction between them.

She was needy. We know she was needy. She had not yet quite gotten over the James Nathan episode. And he? We will never know for sure. Why Margaret, of all people? Then again, why not? She was an American woman—always a bit exotic to Italian men. He spoke no English. He was barely literate even in Italian. He could not read her books, or her dispatches, or anything she or anyone she was interested in would write. The relationship had to proceed on another level. The feeling had to come from another source.

She had mourned James Nathan's departure for more than a year and finally embarked on a European trip herself, hoping somehow to see him. En route to Italy she stopped in London and met Wordsworth (a disappointment) and the Carlyles. Though Emerson had written glowingly to Carlyle of her conversational powers, Carlyle saw to it that he outtalked her.

The Carlyles in turn introduced her to the legendary revolutionary Giuseppe Mazzini, who became a good and loyal friend to Margaret, appreciating her as American men had not, and writing to her, "You do not know how much I esteem and love you." It was not, however, the romantic love she had sought, but one of deep affection, based on her support for his visionary revolutionary organization, "Young Italy," and for his dream of a united Italian Republic.

Margaret and her companions, the Springs, happily set out to help Mazzini (under death sentence in exile) smuggle himself into Italy with a false American passport, and when he couldn't escape the police who had him under surveillance, couriered letters for him to Rome, where Mama Mazzini made them welcome.

But first, they stopped in Paris, where Margaret met one of her female idols, George Sand, dressed in a gown of violet silk, and Sand's lover, Frédéric Chopin, played his pianoforte for her. In Paris, too, she met Emerson's admirer, and Chopin's countryman, the Polish poet and revolutionary leader, Adam Mickiewicz, who was also, like Mazzini, in exile. Outside Paris, he had a mad wife and two children. In Paris, Louis Philippe had just dismissed him from his position as Professor of Slavic Literature at the Collège de France. He was dangerous. He was also attractive, courageous, and intellectual. Mickiewicz had great respect for Margaret, "the only woman to whom it has been given to touch what is decisive in the present world and to have a presentiment of the world of the future."

So there is Margaret, finally in Europe, writing ultimately from Rome to Emerson:

> I find how true was the lure that always drew me towards Europe. It was no false instinct that said I might here find an atmosphere to develop me in ways I need. Had I only come ten years earlier! Now my life must be a failure, so much strength has been wasted on abstractions, which only came because I grew not in the right soil. However it is a less failure than most others, and not worth thinking twice about.

She was finally on the right soil. She had finally met some men who were so strong and accomplished in themselves, they were not intimidated by her, or perhaps, as Europeans, had a more liberated view at that time of the freedoms available to an educated and forceful woman.

From Rome, she continued to write to Mickiewicz, who tried to convince her not to confine her life:

> ... to books and reveries ... You have pleaded the liberty of woman in a masculine and frank style. Live and act, as you write ... Do not forget that even in your private life as a woman you have rights to maintain. Emerson says rightly: give *all for love*, but this *love* must not be that of the shepherds of Florian nor that of schoolboys and German ladies. The relationships that suit you are those which develop and free your spirit, responding to the legitimate needs of your organism and leaving you free at all times.

In other words, as he said elsewhere, "For you the first step of your deliverance ... is to know, whether you are permitted to remain a virgin."

We do not know if Mickiewicz offered his services in that department. Most probably not. In some ways, he had Margaret on his own kind of pedestal, and was, in any case otherwise involved at that moment, with another woman by whom he had a child. But he divined a need in her, a need stemming from that Eros that Emerson had thought abandoned. He encouraged her to take a lover, and suggested that she feel, recognize, experience, her own beauty.

BEAUTY. No one had ever suggested to her that she could

be beautiful. The suggestion itself was enough for her to toy with the idea of returning to Paris to attach herself to him in an amative sense. Given half a chance, she would have. He affected her, she wrote, "like music or the richest landscape, my heart beat with joy that he at once felt beauty in me also. When I was with him I was happy; and thus far the attraction is so strong that all the way from Paris I felt as if I . . . should return at this moment and leave Italy unseen."

But then, Ossoli appeared, and what she took from Mickiewicz was his advice, which encouraged her to "Prolong your good moments. Do not leave those who would like to remain near you. This is in reference to the little Italian you met in the Church."

18

I am in further despair over my relationship with James Apthorp. Am I in love with him? I don't know. I only know that I am jealous of the Baywatch girl, and it is affecting even my intellectual friendship with James.

In the library, I find it hard to concentrate. I am researching Margaret and Ossoli, Margaret and Italy, as further extensions of my research on Margaret and love. She loved Italy. She found Rome "The City of the Soul." But how did she love Ossoli? What was the nature of that love? While I wonder about this, I find myself dwelling on images of James Apthorp and the Baywatch girl.

The Girl: Long wavy hair falls gently upon her shoulders. There is, of course, a whole sexual iconography for women with long wavy hair. Munch painted them surrounded by sperm. Is the Baywatch girl surrounded by sperm? By

James's sperm? Is she more erotic because she has such long wavy hair? More feminine? More attractive to men? To James Apthorp, particularly?

My hair, my short hair, grows very slowly. I am letting it grow, but it is very slooow. Would the Baywatch girl's hair be more important to James than Melville & Margaret? Does she offer him any kind of intellectual chocolate? If chocolate *is* love, then James and I, with our M & M's, certainly have a kind of love.

We take a break in the hall outside the reading room. We start discussing Olson's book on Melville, *Call Me Ishmael.*

JAMES: As Olson said, "The beginning of man was salt sea." We're made of salt sea. That's what was most important about Melville: "the salt of his blood."

ANGELICA: Olson was an old salt himself wasn't he? From Gloucester. Plenty of salt sea.

JAMES: At one point, he writes, "Melville is not Jonathan Edwards." His answer to the angry God was an Ahab, "a man of elements not of sins."

ANGELICA: I always felt Margaret had too much of Jonathan Edwards in her. And Salem. Did you know she had an ancestor from Salem? All that puritan sense of sin. Maybe that's why she was so affronted when James Nathan made a pass.

JAMES: But you tell me she let Ossoli screw her.

ANGELICA: It's hard to know how that happened.

JAMES: How do you think it happened? She was hot for it, your old maid. She was DYING for it.

ANGELICA: God, you are vulgar sometimes! Why do you
always sneer at Margaret?

James doesn't answer. He picks himself up from the stair
he is sitting on and returns to the reading room. I remain
seated for a few minutes more. Even our M & M's are beginning to sour. The chocolate has gone very bitter.

Tonight, as I watch him meet the Baywatch girl again, I
begin to feel like a voyeur. Am I stalking him? But no. Of
course not. When the library closes, he goes his way and I
go mine. I can't help it if I happen to see that he meets his
"appointment." I can't help it if I notice that her breasts
seem artificially enhanced.

But that's expensive. Who is she? Surely not a real
Baywatch girl with enough money for plastic surgery. For
liposuction, while the rest of us starve for the same effect. But
I have never thought about starving before, of dieting even.
Just now. When I want my body to attract James seriously
again. Now, in bed, on the rarer and rarer occasions when he
joins me, he does not seem serious. He seems, I hate to use
the word, PERFUNCTORY. He leaves very soon after. He is not
only hardly affectionate or caring, he is hardly even polite. I
am beginning to get the feeling that he wants to end it, end
US. But I must have the intellectual and emotional suste-
nance of the M & M's. I must be able to talk to him about
Margaret, and consider his problems with Melville. We must
have, at the very least, our intellectual friendship.

After Margaret died, Emerson said Mrs. Spring told him
she had tired of her literary friendships. James Nathan,

surely, had tired of them, or he would not have made a pass. But after she lost him, after he left her, first for the English mistress (pseudo-waif) and finally, as her mother wrote to her in Rome, for the musician he ultimately married, what was the exact moment when she abandoned her dream? It was a dream she had earlier articulated in a letter to Sophia Peabody about her pending marriage to Hawthorne: ". . . to one who cannot think of love merely in the heart, or even in the common destiny of two souls, but as necessarily comprehending intellectual friendship too, it seems the happiest lot imaginable that lies before you."

It was her full dream, "comprehending intellectual friendship," though reading Goethe she had wondered: "How can a woman of genius love & marry? A man of genius will not love her, he wants repose." Was that Margaret's problem, that she did not give sufficient repose to her man of genius? Is that my problem, that with my constant consummation of intellectual M&M's I destroy James Apthorp's repose? What kind of repose does he get with the Baywatch girl? Is she silent, timid, only active in the throes of their lovemaking?

Unexpectedly, uninvitingly, an image of James in bed with the Baywatch girl invades my mind. I cannot brush it away. It is self-articulating, self-sustaining, even self-clarifying. I see them as on a huge cinema screen. My mind has become a cinema screen. She is Marilyn Monroe, Sophia Loren, and Baywatch girl all in one. Her breasts are 36 DDDD, her waist slender, her hips ample, but no more ample than 32, her legs long and thin, free of cellulite. No bumps, no lumps.

Recently, I read that professional models rub coffee grounds on their thighs, then wrap them in plastic, and brush off with loofahs. No small wrinkles or dimples. They are all Venus de Medici, but they do not modestly hide their pudenda. Is the Baywatch girl a model? What is she doing in Cambridge? Why is she not in New York or Los Angeles? What does she want with my James?

Because that is it. He is MINE. I want to say to him, as Margaret said to Sam Ward: "If you love me as I deserve to be loved, you cannot dispense with seeing me." But I must be more silent, less intellectually assertive. I must not argue with him. I must give him repose.

That's it. Repose. Then I shall vanquish the Baywatch girl. I must be very subtle. I must order yet another cantilevered bra from Victoria's Secret. I must try the coffee grounds, especially on my upper thighs. Above all, I must not tell James that I have a new article being published. He has just had another rejected.

19

Margaret in Italy is a totally different problem. She had found the right soil. The Italian soil that nurtured the tall cypresses, the umbrella pines, the leafy Claudian trees, and golden fields of sunflowers now also nurtured Margaret Fuller, who had been drier, more dessicated in the freezing temperatures of Emerson and New England. Before, she had been puritan-dry. Now she began to be juicier, succulent, like the vineyards. Was she ready for a bacchanal?

No. No way. It wasn't quite like that. But she was ready. Ready, surely, for a more sensual, less ideal relationship than she had ever sought. She had already found, possibly for the first time in her life, men who in respecting her mind also found her person attractive. The devotion of the two visionaries, Mazzini and Mickiewicz, suggests that they saw something the American men had missed.

Ask any American woman who has travelled in Europe. They all say the same thing. European men are more aware of them as *women,* regardless of Mind. But, you say, James Nathan was a European. That's just the point. He was aware of her as a woman, but on American soil, with her puritan roots dug deep into home ground, she was affronted at his advances.

Now, in Italy, the ground under her feet has a different feel. Time exists in a different way. She is just a speck here, surrounded by the ruins of successive civilizations going back thousands of years. In Rome she can touch those Ancients she read while still a child. But instead of the blood dreams that followed on reading Virgil, she can dream of aqueducts stepping across the Campagna into infinity, while wild flowers speckle the plain with color. She can enter the Pantheon, see heaven through the oculus, and converse with the Gods and Goddesses who peopled her Boston "Conversations."

At the Miserere of the Sistine Chapel, she sits next to Goethe's daughter-in-law Ottilia, and is introduced to her by Mrs. Jameson. If she follows Goethe to the outskirts of Rome, she can retrace his visit to the Pyramid of Cestus. Then stroll next door to the Protestant Cemetery, to visit Keats, not long dead. Then, back in Rome, stand on the Spanish Steps with so many of the other Americans who cluster around that area and peek into his rooms from the landing. From there, she can join the American and European artists at the Caffè Greco, where her friend Washington Allston sipped his coffee with Coleridge and

Washington Irving more than 40 years earlier, or maybe just slip back to dream some more in the Gardens of the Villa Borghese (in which, when not dreaming, she saves the son of her travelling companions from drowning in a fountain).

The climate she finds "enchanting," the people "indolently joyous," the objects of contemplation "so numerous and admirable that one cannot pass the time better than by quietly looking one's fill." "Rome," she writes to Cary, "must be inhaled wholly, with the yielding of the whole heart. It is really something transcendent, both spirit and body." "Italy," she writes to Elizabeth Hoar, "receives me as a long lost child, and I feel myself at home here."

The child again. The longing to be a child. The same longing she had with James Nathan. Is it because she is tired of being wise, erudite, the great intellectual legend? What is it of the childlike state that draws her? She loves children, adored little Waldo Emerson. When Horace Greeley sends news of his young son Pickie's death, she is distraught. Does she see in the child her own thwarted childhood, that childhood snatched from her by her father, that loss she so regrets that she was ready, with James Nathan, to toss aside the imperious Margaret Fuller and become, as he once called her, "a little girl"?

From her rooms on the Corso, near the Pincian Mount and the Piazza del Popolo where she sits by the fountains, she can see "all that goes on in Rome." Her landlady, a Marchesa by marriage of somewhat dubious reputation, introduces her to her "present lover." Perhaps the lady's own relationship makes her more tolerant of Margaret's, for Ossoli is surely in the picture by now, his presence in Margaret's rooms an accepted fact at her modest Sunday evening at homes (no food, but flowers, for she is very poor) and on other, more private occasions as well.

For a very long time, she does not write home about Ossoli. She has American and European friends in Rome, among them the sculptor, William Wetmore Story and his wife Emelyn, and Christopher Cranch, the artist, poet, and philosopher, whose caricature of Emerson as a transparent eyeball remains one of the wittiest comments on Transcendentalism. About many of these, she has much to say. But of Ossoli her letters home offer hardly a word.

The right soil is growing a different Margaret-plant. Something else has taken root, something that will be a stranger flower, no longer the Agnus Castus. Margaret no longer wants to be doomed to live in the cold, without love. Warmed by the Italian sun, Margaret wants now to be infused with the sensual juice of life. Ossoli is there, and she is ready for him. Her books are no longer a substitute, her intellect no longer offers full satisfaction. With Ossoli, almost totally unschooled, lacking in intellect, in language, in ideas, in anything but the simple joy of walks in the country and bread and wine feasts, she can finally drop her intellect because she is forced to. She has no choice. He cannot meet her on the most elementary level of verbal communication. He knows no English. He can barely read Italian.

So. No mind. No ideas. No intellect. No language. Powerful sacrifices for the woman who dominates American letters more than any other member of her sex in the decade before her death. And what does she get in return? What has she always wanted?

Someone who wants *her.* Who finds her desirable. Who makes her feel, finally, like a woman who is loved. Romantically. Devotedly.

How does her seduction take place? Is it something that happens to Margaret wilfully, with full cognizance of Mickiewicz's suggestion that she take full charge of her life by terminating her virgin state? To Mickiewicz, Ossoli was the "little Italian you met in the church." And to Margaret, what was he? A vehicle, a deliberately chosen accessory in her plan to accelerate her womanly freedom on European shores? She likes the fact that he is ten years younger. He reminds her of her brother Eugene. Is the familial resemblance pivotal? She had begged Nathan to allow her to be his sister. But remember, she had cited the brother/sister relationships that Wordsworth and Byron had with their siblings. Are there also incestuous overtones in the resemblance of Ossoli to Eugene?

On this issue, Margaret always seems innocent. But she is not thoroughly innocent. Else, the conception of little Nino would not have taken place. She is innocent enough to conceive, however, and not know how to prevent it. No pills. No diaphragms. I am myself ignorant of the birth control methods available in Italy in 1847. I suspect she is, too. But it is also possible that she hears her biological clock chiming. She loves children. She wants a child of her own.

Does she choose Ossoli the way Madonna (our Madonna, not the holy one) chose the father of little Lourdes? She is 37. She wants to be a mother. And Eros, the same Eros painted by Thomas Hicks when she posed for him while secretly pregnant, Eros, according to Jung, is maternal. The child, when she has him, is "a source of ineffable joys, far purer, deeper than anything I ever felt before, like what Nature had sometimes given, but more intimate, more sweet."

So Ossoli achieves what James Nathan has not. Ossoli becomes her lover. By December 1847, she has conceived. And when she discovers her pregnancy, still keeping her news largely to herself, she falls into a deep depression.

Does this mean she has *not* wanted the child? Not necessarily. It's hard to be overjoyed, even about a child you have yearned for, when you are unmarried, poor, involved in a secret relationship with someone your snobby intellectual friends will look down on. It is not, after all, the 1990s, when movie stars and models decide with impunity to be single mothers. Her roots are puritan. And even in Italy, a bastard is a bastard, though Bastardo is also the name of a place.

The story goes that Ossoli asked for her hand early in their relationship. She turned him down, for all the obvious reasons. But when she finds herself pregnant, they still do not marry right away (if ever). And it is raining. It rains in Rome for months. She loves Rome, but the weather, added to the pregnancy, is more than she can bear. She still has her mind. But now it is only a part of her. Something else has been added.

20

My head is in two places. I feel like my brain is split in half. I am with Margaret and Ossoli in Italy. I am with James Apthorp in Boston and Cambridge.

Sitting in Houghton with Margaret's papers, I can visualize her in Italy. Margaret was so right about the Mind. It is invisible. Intangible. Without color. Without weight. Yet Mind can travel. THOUGHT can bring me to Italy so vividly that I can feel the warmth of the Italian sun sitting here in the library. I can travel back almost 150 years and sit beside her in a carriage as she drives along the Pincio, looking out over the prospect of Rome, over the dome of St.Peter's, her favorite place, her symbolic place, the place where she met Ossoli. I can eat with them, an uninvited, unexpected, unsuspected guest as they dine modestly on roasted chestnuts and bread and wine from inexpensive osterias. I can wander with them into the Palazzo Barberini, where the American expatriates love to rent rooms, and crane my neck to look up at the extraordinary baroque ceiling of Pietro da Cortona, with figures flying out of the air, as though they will drop on us, all dotted with Barberini papal bees. I can climb with them up the Spanish Steps to the Trinità dei Monte, with its distinctive pylon. I can join them on excursions into the countryside along the infinite flat plain of the Roman Campagna, strewn with wild flowers, speckled with ancient tombs, and then cross over to Albano or Castel Gandolfo, where the Pope has a summer palace, all in the golden sunshine which still warms my head and shoulders as I sit in this room that houses her thoughts and dreams.

But things are hotting up in Rome, too, politically. Pius IX has just begun his reign over the Papal States as a reformer, well liked by liberals. Italy is a confusion of separate states with a king, Charles Albert, ruling Piedmont-Sardinia, an Austrian army occupying Lombardy and Venetia, and a Bourbon king, Ferdinand, ruling Naples, also known as the Kingdom of the Two Sicilies.

In 1848, there are revolutions all over Europe. In February, the French revolution topples King Louis Philippe. In March, the Austrians push out Prince Metternich. But the Italian situation is the one that involves Margaret, and has involved her mind and heart since she first met Mazzini (who will soon be in Rome, along with Mickiewicz) in London with the Carlyles. Austria is the chief Italian oppressor, and the Milanese first revolt against Austrian tobacco taxes. It is not quite like the Americans and the

Boston Tea Party, with John Singleton Copley's father-in-law's tea landing in Boston Harbor, but for Margaret, it must be close enough. She keeps hoping the new Pope will lead the way to Italy's united freedom. She keeps sending her dispatches to the *Tribune* about the latest developments. But the Pope disappoints her, and rejects the idea of committing Roman troops against Austria, and the idea of an Italian republic as well.

The disappointment is not only about her hopes for Italy. It has direct bearing on her relation with Ossoli. His family is committed to the Pope, with long papal ties. He has joined the Civic Guard, which the Pope permits to be formed as a concession to the Roman people, and when his loyalties are tested, he stands with the now liberal Civic Guard for the revolution, even against the Pope, who ultimately flees Rome, returning only after the failure of the five-month-old republic when the French army comes in to restore him.

As all these events are developing, Margaret continues to send dispatches to Greeley's *Tribune*, which has been paying her for them, and she dearly needs money, not ashamed even to ask for monetary assistance from friends who have more than she has.

But I can picture her growing fatter. Beginning to show and trying still to conceal it. What kind of maternity clothes were available then? How full could her costumes be to mask the bump of the growing fetus? She still does not want anyone to know. But Mickiewicz, when he arrives, takes rooms near hers, soon discovers her condition, and tells her it is "natural."

By the end of May she leaves, and goes first to Aquila, and finally to Rieti for the birth. She is in seclusion, so much so that the sympathetic Italians call her *povera, sola, soletta*. They wash her clothes in the stream and feed her turnip broth.

She writes to Ossoli short, practical, informational letters. Please send newspapers: "I know nothing about the things that I am interested in; I feel lonely, imprisoned, too unhappy. . . ."

Then the newspapers arrive: "I suppose twenty newspapers altogether . . . It doesn't rain; it is terribly hot . . . If it is not inconvenient to you, I want you to get me at Soave's, Piazza di Spagna, a bottle of their excellent Cologne price 5 paoli."

There are no philosophical ideas here. Their relationship is commonplace, what she often referred to earlier as "domestic." She has not always wanted that, but it is what she has.

The letters, written in Italian, are addressed *Mio Caro*, and sometimes *Mio Amore*. After the child is born on September 5th (a Virgo, a Virgo, triumph of the Virgin after all), she calls Ossoli finally *Cmo Consorte*—Dearest Husband.

When do they marry? Where and how? Do they?

Some have suggested the April before. Some, after the child's birth. She is a Protestant, he a Catholic. They are by now in the middle of a war. How do they get a special dispensation? Do they? Can they?

James enters the library and sits opposite me, at the table, catching my eye and nodding brusquely. He plunks his papers down and gets into his work right away. I feel his emotional and mental distance.

What do I do about James? He still comes on occasion to my bed, but grudgingly. I try to be more open, more giving, sexually. To still my mind when I am with him, to be more reposeful. I watch him now as he is absorbed in his work. I watch his fine-boned face, his intent blue eyes, his mouth pursed in thought, the graceful movement of his slender fingers as he turns a page. Where is he in Melville tonight? Is Melville still depressed?

I could talk to him about Margaret's depression, which finally lifts after three months of Roman rain. When she writes, almost ecstatically, in April: "The Gods themselves walk on earth, here in the Italian Spring. Day after day of sunny weather lights up the flowery glades and Arcadian woods. The fountains, hateful during the endless rains, charm again. At Castle Fusano I found heaths in full flower. I felt cheered. Such beauty is irresistible." But then, she remembers, she is still pregnant: ". . . the drama of my fate is very deep and the ship plunges deeper as it rises higher." Still pregnant. That does not lift. So we could still discuss depression. And weather.

How weather affects the mind and soul. How even weather can cause depression. Is that why we all watch the Weather Channel on TV so avidly? To see whether we will be depressed by the weather that day? It is not only a matter of getting wet, ruining one's hair or clothes, even catching cold. It is a matter of state of mind, and possibly of depression.

They are finding out a lot about depression, about chemical causes, about serotonin, or whether one has taken enough Vitamin B. Some people take St. John's Wort. But what can Margaret take for her depression? She is pregnant, and can hardly tell anyone. Boston society, with its puritan roots would at the least gossip about, if not reject her. With my head half in Italy, and my body in New England, what connection do I have with puritan roots? I am myself half-Italian. I have no puritan roots. But I am born an American. American society is grounded in puritan roots. Does that give me puritan roots by default? Do I have any access at all to puritan roots?

James does. James is firmly rooted. James has pure puritan roots. But then, why is he involved with the Baywatch girl? Is he like that earlier Puritan, Cotton Mather, who passed judgment on witches but loved little girls? If I leave Houghton now and walk out into the Cambridge night, I can still see umbrella pines and cypresses along the Pincio. James would remain in the cool, dry air of New England, his most sensuous contact, perhaps, with the Baywatch girl. But I, on the other hand, can still feel the warm sun of Italy on my head, and taste the juice of Italian grapes, though to everyone else I am simply walking through Harvard Square.

As it happens, we leave together. The Baywatch girl seems to be absent tonight. I am encouraged. We stop for a cup of coffee. He is anxious tonight to talk about Melville. Ah. He is offering me some of our M & M's. Our intellectual chocolate love. I accept gladly, and hope he is noticing my new cantilevered bra, which has arrived via UPS from Victoria's Secret. We are back to Hawthorne, which suits me, since I am still convinced that Hawthorne's rejection of his love was the cause of much of Melville's depression. And Hawthorne's connection with Margaret is peculiar, since he repudiated their friendship after her death, but seems to have had a love/hate relationship with Zenobia/Priscilla in *The Blithedale Romance*.

JAMES: Hawthorne was bloody well embarrassed by Melville. Melville's letters to him were practically love letters.

He is toying with his coffee cup. For the first time in a long time, he seems relaxed, willing to loiter over our M & M's. The absence of the Baywatch girl clearly has opened the path for my presence. For our M & M's to emerge naturally, to flow in our conversation.

ANGELICA: Hawthorne seems to have had very set ideas
about sex and gender. Same-sex relationships frightened
him.
JAMES: (*Looking at me darkly*) Don't they frighten *you*?

I feel an argument coming on. I must not be assertive, not even in the middle of our M & M's, which are, after all, intellectual discussions, and can tolerate some assertiveness. But now I am afraid. I must not rock the boat. Must not open the door to the Baywatch girl. I must defer to James. I must squelch my instinct to take offense, to defend myself.

I thrust out my newly cantilevered breasts. I watch his eyes go to them. Good. They are having their effect. I change the subject, deftly I hope, from same-sex relationships to marriage. The orthodoxy of it should appeal to James's puritan roots.

ANGELICA: What was Hawthorne's relation to his wife Sophia?

JAMES: Sophia was a piece of work.

ANGELICA: What does *that* mean?

JAMES: When he first met her, she was a semi-invalid. She would only eat white bread, white meat, milk. I suppose it supported the idea of her purity. Hawthorne was nuts about purity. All his blonde Anglo-Saxon women were pure. He called her his Dove. She called him Apollo. She wrote to her sister: "Apollo boiled some potatoes for breakfast."

ANGELICA: Was it a good marriage?

JAMES (*suspiciously*): What's a good marriage? She let him be The Man. She was a bit of an artist—a copyist, and a sensitive writer. But he was delighted when she turned down a chance to publish her writing because it would interfere with being the best wife and mother. Of course, he resented the kids because they took her away from him. Still, he got her full admiration and devotion. He was her God. Melville also saw him as Apollonian. Sophia, you know, was intrigued by Melville's eyes, which surprised her because she said they were very small to see so much. She talked about his "strange lazy glance" which she felt had unique power. I don't think she ever copped on to the fact that Melville was pursuing her husband, even though he dedicated *Moby-Dick* to him, and, twenty-five years later in his long poem, "Clarel," he wrote about Hawthorne as Vine "so feminine his passionate mood," and talked about "that repulsed advance" and his (Clarel's) still hungering, unsatisfied heart.

ANGELICA: Poor Melville. He didn't have as many rejections as Margaret, but Hawthorne's rejection went deep.

JAMES: I'm still not sure how deep. He missed the guy stuff—drinking champagne and smoking cigars together, but I never knew whether Hawthorne left Lenox so abruptly in 1851 because of Melville's advances or not. Hawthorne and Sophia had intended on staying another two years. Melville bought the place in Arrowhead, only six miles away, shortly after they met in 1850.

ANGELICA: When in 1850?

JAMES: It was a famous day, their meeting: August 5th.

ANGELICA: God. Margaret drowned less than three weeks earlier, on July 19th.

JAMES: Margaret's friend, Cary, gets into the act, too.

ANGELICA: Cary? Her long-time same-sex relationship? Are we back to that again?

JAMES: It's just that her husband, William Tappan, was Hawthorne's landlord. Sophia was away for a few weeks, and evidently Cary also made a pass at him. So I don't know whether Cary or Melville caused Hawthorne's sudden departure.

ANGELICA: Hawthorne seems to have been afraid of both men *and* women.

JAMES: Everyone but Sophia. They were very reclusive. They called their sexual relations "blissful interviews." I like what she said: "Behold a true wife's world! It is her husband only." That's a gal after my own heart.

(*James laughs but I think he means it.*)

ANGELICA: Really?

JAMES: She wasn't trying to be a *man,* like your Margaret.

I start to answer and stop. I must still my voice.

James, expecting a retort, looks smug about getting the last word. Tonight he comes to my bed, but it is not quite a "blissful interview." He still does not seem to have his heart in it. He leaves quickly.

Natasha Owens has been in touch. She has called, getting my machine, and left little notes for me, delivered by hand. As I think of it, it feels like a bit more than "in touch." She says she would like to continue pursuing our "whole relationship." She says I cannot have a "whole" relationship with a man, because he is Other.

How Other is James Apthorp? He still seems to be enjoying at least some of our M & M's, though he enjoys them more if I don't disagree with him. He is still touchy about Melville and Hawthorne. He's willing to admit Melville had a thing for Hawthorne, but not that Hawthorne's rejection caused Melville's depression.

James's rejection is beginning to cause MY depression. He

comes to my bed only occasionally now, still perfunctorily, as though he is doing me a favor. Even the new cantilevered bra only holds his interest for so long. Once it is off, he seems not to care any more. Maybe I should leave it on. Maybe that would help. I can't seem to excite any passion in him, and though I was not that passionate myself initially, I find myself more so now. I want him to find me attractive, to desire me, to love me with passion.

Natasha Owens clearly wants to love me with passion, but I still find a same-sex relationship hard. Before Margaret, I never even conceived of it. Natasha tells me I don't know what I am missing, that the "fullness, the wholeness, the total understanding of it," of me as a woman, would be greater than anything with James.

I will have dinner at her apartment next week. I am willing to try to pursue a "whole relationship," but I am put off by the idea of same-sex sex. I don't quite know what it involves, what I'm supposed to do.

21

After the baby's birth, Margaret leaves him in Rieti with an Italian family, while she returns to Rome and revolution. In Rome, she now has only one large room: ". . . everything about the bed so gracefully and adroitly disposed that it makes a beautiful parlor, and of course I pay much less. I have the sun all day, and an excellent chimney. It is very high and has pure air, and the most beautiful view all around."

From her room, she can see the Piazza Barberini and the Pope's palace. The Marchesa of doubtful reputation has been replaced by an old couple. The three dogs of her former landlady replaced by a black cat called Amoretto.

But Rome is increasingly violent. Rossi, a much-hated repressive minister, is assassinated on the steps of the Chamber of Deputies, and no one is sorry, not even Margaret, who is generally compassionate: "I never thought to have heard of a violent death with satisfaction, but this act affected me as one of terrible justice."

The Pope has let the people down. The troops and people confront his Swiss Guards while he hides inside his palace. "It is almost impossible for anyone to act," she writes, "unless the Pope is stripped of his temporal power, and the hour for that is not yet quite ripe; though they talk more and more of proclaiming the Republic, and even of calling my friend Mazzini." The Pope flees Rome in late November.

Margaret returns to Rieti to check on the baby when she can, and reports to Ossoli that he "has charming habits . . . I have given him all your kisses." In December, when the baby is almost four months old, she writes, "He plays often with the little donkey. He still does not have any hair."

Though in December she shares news of the child with Cary, she extracts from her a promise of secrecy.

Back in Rome in January, she writes to her brother:

> Yesterday as I went forth I saw the house where Keats lived in Rome where he died. I saw the Casino of Raphael. Returning I passed the Villa where Goethe lived when in Rome; afterwards the houses of Claude and Poussin . . . I live myself in the apartment described in Andersen's "Improvisatore." I have the room, I suppose, indicated as being occupied by the Danish Sculptor.

She is still allowing her family to think of her as someone on a Grand Tour, soaking up the important sites and monuments.

To Emerson, she writes, "I am leading a lonely life here in Rome which seems my Rome this winter." No word yet to him, her icicle, of Ossoli's existence. Yet she sees Ossoli as often as she can, while her family and friends (Cary and Mickiewicz excepted) know nothing of the child, or of the marriage she might or might not have contracted.

By March, Mazzini is welcomed back to Rome as a Roman citizen—with prospects of being President of the Republic. Things are hotting up. Garibaldi's legion is near Rieti and Neapolitan troops are six miles off. She is disturbed by this, but writes to Cary about little Nino: "All the solid happiness I have known has been at times when he went to sleep in my arms."

Jung's Maternal Eros, fulfilled at last.

By the end of March, the French are authorized to invade Italy as a move against Austria. They claim to be on a mission to save the Roman republic, but nobody believes them. In April, the Roman Assembly elects a government to be led by a triumvirate that includes Mazzini, who moves into rooms in the Quirinal Palace, near Margaret. By the end of April, the French have attacked Rome, and Margaret moves into the Casa Diez on Via Gregoriana, along with the Storys and other Americans who are sheltered there by the American government.

An Italian friend, Princess Belgioioso, asks her to direct the volunteer nurses at the Hospital of Fate Bene Fratelli. She works in the hospital throughout the battle for the defense of Rome. She is anxious about Ossoli, who is now heavily engaged in that defense with the Civic Guard:

"Please do not fail to see me, it is terrible to spend so many anxious hours without seeing you again."

By the end of May, she writes to her brother:

> The Neapolitans have been driven back but the French seem to be amusing us with a pretense of treaties, while waiting for the Austrians to come up. The Austrians cannot, I suppose, be more than three days march from us. I feel but little about myself. Such thoughts are merged in indignation, and the fears I have that Rome may be bombarded . . . I am with William Story, his wife and uncle, very kind friends . . . They are going away, so soon as they can find horses—going into Germany. I remain alone in the house, under our flag, almost the only American, except the Consul and Ambassador.

Before they leave for Germany, Margaret confides in Emelyn Story, gives her documents in the event of her death, and asks that little Nino be sent, if both she and Ossoli die, to the care of her mother and Cary. Roughly half a century later, writing about William Wetmore Story and his friends, Henry James refers to Margaret as the "Margaret-ghost."

They have cut down the great trees in the Borghese Gardens to make barricades. They have closed the museums. Now here, in Italy, Margaret has replaced James Nathan with Giovanni Ossoli. She has stood by him as he fought for Rome. She has stood by the Romans, whom she now feels are her own people, even as she takes shelter under the American flag while resting from her hospital duties. Her voice, once stilled by James Nathan as she begged ignominiously for his love, is now raised eloquently in favor of the Republic in the dispatch letters she is sending to Greeley's *Tribune*.

Her letters to Ossoli indicate what they share:

> How sorry I am, love, to miss you yesterday and possibly also today: if you can come, I go to Casa Diez, if possible inquire for me there, on the last floor, if I am still there or if I went to the hospital. God keep you. How much I suffered at the sight of those wounded people, and I have no way of knowing whether something happens to you, but one must hope, I received the letter from Rieti, Our Nino is perfectly well, thanks for this. It does me good that at least the Romans have done something, if only you can survive.

Rome is critically attacked by the French on June 3rd. The city is under siege. By June 6th, Margaret writes to Emelyn Story:

> I witnessed a terrible battle . . . It began at four in the morning; it lasted to the last gleam of light. The musket fire was almost unintermitted, the roll of the cannon, especially from St. Angelo, most majestic . . . I saw the smoke of every discharge, the flash of the bayonets . . . The French throw rockets into the town; one burst in the court-yard of the hospital, just as I arrived there yesterday, agitating the poor sufferers very much; they said they did not want to die like mice in a trap.

22

Natasha Owens' apartment is orderly as usual. For some reason, I find this reassuring. My head has been with Margaret in the midst of all the Roman bombardment, and the clean precision of the apartment on Commonwealth Avenue grounds me again, for the moment at least, in Boston. It was, after all, Boston where Margaret held her "Conversations" for the New England ladies. Conversations where Margaret could ask her women friends, "What is Life?" and speak herself, finally, having heard their answers, of God as spirit, Life, so full as to create and love eternally:

> . . . Love and creativeness are dynamic forces, out of which we, individually, as creatures go forth bearing his image, that is, having within our being the same dynamic forces, by which we add constantly to the sum of existence, and shaking off ignorance, and its effects, and by becoming

more ourselves, i.e., more divine;—destroying sin in its principle, we attain to absolute freedom, we return to God, conscious like himself, and as his friends, giving, as well as receiving, felicity forevermore. In short, we become Gods.

As Boston Gods, or Goddesses, women with intellectual proclivities could attend Margaret's classes and commune with other women with similar heads (and hearts). Let us not forget the hearts. Melville said to Hawthorne, "I'm with the hearts, to the dogs with the heads." But Margaret and her women wanted it all. Heart and head. To be a woman and be allowed, *allowed* to use intellect. Without being called a man. Without being resented by men. Without having to please the patriarchy by denying the *whole* self.

Ossoli didn't resent Margaret's intellect, because, having little or none of his own, he couldn't recognize hers, even if it were in his own language. So she had sidestepped the Big Problem. The problem she couldn't really sidestep with James Nathan. The problem I have not been able to sidestep with *my* James. My James enjoys our M & M's, but he does not relate to me, I am sure, as he does to the Baywatch girl. The M & M's get in the way. *Intellect* gets in the way. A strange male aversion to equal intellect gets in the way. If I were sexier, my hair longer, my breasts larger still, not just cantilevered but enlarged, would that help? Do I need silicon implants to make James passionate about me?

Natasha Owens seems passionate about me without the silicon. She sits me down on her couch and offers me some white wine. She asks about Margaret. She seems genuinely interested. This is surely part of the "whole relationship" thing. That we can share both heart and head.

NATASHA: Margaret's problem was that for all her radical progressivism, for all her feminism, she still bought into the idea of romantic love with a man. What a crock!

ANGELICA: Well, she was mad about Anna Barker, but Anna married Sam Ward. Not only that, she talked him into being a banker, into being about *money*, instead of being an artist. Margaret didn't like that. And Cary, of course, remained a friend, but didn't even tell Margaret when she was getting married. Margaret was hurt by that.

NATASHA: So she wanted to get married too. That's the gist of it. She fell into the whole marriage trap, after all she'd written against it.

ANGELICA: It was more the baby, I think. She was pushed by her Maternal Eros. Jung got it right. Maybe all female Eros is basically maternal. We're nurturers.

NATASHA: If you married me, we could still have children. Same-sex marriages can do that now. Just pick out your stud, and implant his semen. You can have a child without having to put up with a man.

ANGELICA: Oh, Natasha. Look, I like you very much. But I'm totally heterosexual.

NATASHA: (*suddenly leaping over to the couch from the armchair in which she is sitting*) Are you quite sure?

She has grabbed me again, as she did the first time. Now she pins me down on the couch, and jumps on top of me.

She starts rubbing herself against me, rubbing our two mounds and our four breasts together. I am beginning to get aroused. This is crazy. And interesting. It is a kind of mutual masturbation. Later I discover it has a name: Tribadism. Now she has pushed her tongue into my mouth again. White wines mixing. I try not to respond. I push her away. I am both attracted and repelled. We are in Boston. Is this the beginning of a Boston marriage?

Since that's what it's called, there must have been a lot of those in Boston. Home of the Puritans and of the sisters in Lesbos. Above the flesh. But Natasha is not being above the flesh. She is trying to get into my flesh. Her fingers are grabbing under my skirt. I push her away. I stand up.

ANGELICA: Is this the whole relationship you've been talking about? It doesn't feel like a whole relationship to me. It's the same old thing. Sex, sex sex. God! It's all the same thing.

NATASHA: Angelica . . . Angelica . . . Admit your sexuality. Let it go!

I look at her with her short hair and small breasts. I think of James and the Baywatch girl. I want to be like the Baywatch girl.

I leave before dinner, almost tempted by the aroma of the leg of lamb she is preparing. But I don't want a whole relationship with a woman. I want it with a man. I want it with *that* man. I want James.

23

By June 30th, the revolution is over. The French will enter Rome on July 3rd. Garibaldi leaves with his followers and will end up—while in temporary exile—making candles on Staten Island. Mazzini makes his way out to Switzerland, Mickiewicz to Paris. Margaret's two great visionary friends: vanquished and dispersed. "The last American left," she leaves Rome on July 12th for Rieti, where she finds little Nino wasted away, ill and neglected. Margaret devotes herself to nursing him back to health. Ossoli joins her in August, and they are finally reunited as a family. She is now willing to be known as "Marchesa Ossoli". She is now willing to reveal her secret to her family and friends. Her son, she says, will inherit the title of Marchese.

In *Woman in the Nineteenth Century* she had written that, the "highest grade of marriage" includes "intellectual communion, for how sad it would be on such a journey to have a companion to whom you could not communicate thoughts and aspirations as they sprang to life. . . . "

Now she is on that sad journey. Now she makes it clear that "the time was gone when I could more than *prefer* any man. Yet I shall never regret the step which has given me the experience of a mother and satisfied domestic wants in a most sincere and sweet companion."

Ossoli is her "gentle friend, ignorant of great ideas, ignorant of books, enlightened as to his duties by pure sentiment and an unspoiled nature. . . ."

IGNORANT! She does not hesitate to call him ignorant, but not ignorant as a human being, ignorant simply of books and ideas. *Simply*? This is the woman who had said she would suffocate without books. Her heart, however would also have suffocated "without a child of my own."

On several occasions, and to several different confidantes, she compares him to violets. Are we back once more in her mother's garden? A nineteenth-century floral dictionary describes violets as "true friends. We do not know half their sweetness till they have felt the sunshine of our kindness . . . they are like the pleasures of our childhood, the earliest and the most beautiful."

To her mother, she writes:

> He is not in any respect such a person as people in general would expect to find with me. He had no instructor except an old priest, who entirely neglected his education; and of all that is contained in books he is absolutely ignorant, and he has no enthusiasm of character. On the other hand, he

has excellent practical sense . . . has a nice sense of duty . . . a very sweet temper, and great native refinement. His love for me has been unswerving and most tender. I have never suffered a pain that he could relieve. His devotion, when I am ill, is to be compared only with yours . . . In him I have found a home, and one that interferes with no tie. Amid many ills and cares, we have had much joy together, in the sympathy with natural beauty, with our child, with all that is innocent and sweet.

INNOCENCE. TENDERNESS. DEVOTION. SWEETNESS. Ossoli offers UNSWERVING LOVE.

Does this sound like what one expects of a dog?

Am I being hard on her? Did she, as they say, *settle*? She has waited so long for someone to love her, and even with Ossoli, she fears she might be a bit too old. That, as the younger, he could stop loving her. Even with him, she does not feel fully lovable. But for now she has the violet, and the child, and both create a state of innocence. Does this state redeem in her puritan mind the lost virginity? The scandal of the only-maybe marriage, the mysterious nuptial the circumstances of which are still never mentioned?

To Anna Barker, her Récamier, and Anna's husband Samuel Ward, both of whom she loved and lost, she writes that her "husband" is:

> . . . entirely without what is commonly called culture . . . nature has been his book . . . To me the simplicity, the reality, the great tenderness and refinement of his character make a domestic place in this world and as it is

for my heart that he loves me, I hope he may always be able to feel the same, but that is as God pleases.

Does she indeed trade head for heart, intellect for feeling, culture for nature, ideas and language for "a domestic place in this world"? It is not quite *kinder, kirche, küche,* but it seems close. Has she traded some ideal of romantic passion for gentleness? Cultural sophistication for natural innocence? Is it a kind of Rousseauian primitivism she seeks? Was she an Italian nymph to Ossoli's satyr? Is that how it happened, the initial seduction? The ultimate begetting of little Nino? But there is really nothing abandoned and bacchanalian about this romance. It is not a revel by Rubens, or worse, Jordaens. Titian then? A bit more restrained?

No. Not a revel at all. It is Jung's Eros, the maternal compulsion, the biological necessity, the child, the child, she wants *the child.*

And to beget the child with the aid of an innocent is to double the innocence. To yield only to nature, and then not nature in its wild state, but the gentle violet of nature. The surrender of culture becomes itself a form of redemption through traffic with Ossoli's ignorant innocence.

But oh, hear this, hear this, is it total surrender? Elsewhere she writes "the tie leaves me mentally free." She can have it all. MIND is still there.

The Gemini heroine has simply been split into her two zodiacal parts. One twinned self is Nature/Anima/Feeling. One is Culture/Animus/Intellect.

She writes to the Wards from Florence, where she and her little family have retreated, but her heart is in Rome, where Ossoli, as part of the revolutionary force, is now *persona non grata*. "It is not Florence I would have chosen to touch." Florence, she says, "is a kind of Boston; it has not the poetic greatness of the other Italian cities; it is a place to work and study in; simple life does not seem so great." The air agrees with the baby, but still Florence does not charm her, and she is homesick for Rome. She cannot understand why the Brownings would want to live in Florence when they could live in Rome.

She may, of course, be quite right about Florence. Florence is to Rome as Boston is to New York or Dublin to London. And surprise, surprise, since they are now in a place to work and study in: "Ossoli is forming some taste for books, which I never expected, also he is studying English." Is some strange reversal going on, of the kind that can happen between husband and wife? Is she becoming more natural, more, in a sense, primitive? Is it possible that he is acquiring a veneer of culture?

But it can only be a slim veneer, and given the language difficulty, not even really that. Does he now open the covers of books and wonder what could possibly be inside them? What the strange markings, the hieroglyphs mean? The code of civilized communication? Language?

He does not get too far along, cannot get far along in the short time left to them on earth. They have less than a year to live. He has, in any case, breathed "something of the violet" into her life.

24

My work is nearing completion. I have stretched the department's patience to its limit. John Denton reminds me that I must submit my book for tenure review within the month. When I stop at the departmental office to consult with him, Bill Lipton is there, leering at me, suggesting dinner. He has done this before, virtually every time we meet, but it feels a bit different now.

BILL LIPTON: Angelica, don't you think you should take some time off? I know you're feeling rushed, but how about dinner at my place? You can bounce some of your ideas off me—maybe it would help.

ANGELICA (*sweetly*): What a lovely suggestion. But I'm really feeling pressed. Maybe after I've submitted my manuscript to the department.

BILL LIPTON (*slowly, with significant pauses*): It might be more
helpful to you if we met before.

Is it an implied threat? Sexual blackmail? If I sleep with
Bill Lipton do I get his vote?

And how about Natasha Owens? Have I lost her vote by
not eating her dinner? Why is all this sexual politicking
entering into academic politicking? Academic politicking, as
everyone knows, is even worse than Washington politicking.
Add sex to it and it goes off the charts.

I try to turn Bill Lipton off with a smile. He looks a bit
miffed, but I don't stop to pacify him. I am on my way to
Houghton.

I leave the building. It is a few minutes before I realize that
Natasha Owens is trailing behind me at a discreet distance.
She seems to be making no effort to catch up. Perhaps it is
just a coincidence that she is going in the same direction.

I lose her when I descend into the cars to Cambridge,
but this evening when I leave Houghton, I think I notice
her short dark hair and black jeans trailing me again. Her
white sneakers pick up the light. I am too busy to stop and
ask if she is indeed following me, because tonight, for the
first time, I am following James Apthorp and the Baywatch
girl. In the dark of evening, Natasha is tracking me and I
am tracking James. Have we begun to play some kind of
stalking game? No. It is simply a kind of serial tracking. It
is harmless. It is done out of curiosity. I want to know
where James Apthorp goes with the Baywatch girl. And

Natasha? Maybe she wants to know why I did not eat her leg of lamb.

It is not that difficult to follow James and the Baywatch girl without being noticed. They seem to have eyes only for each other. They cross Harvard Yard arm in arm under the tall trees. They hold hands. Their bodies seem always to touch. To connect. James does not walk that way with me. We always have some small distance between us. He does not put his arm around my shoulder. He does not stop and embrace me, hug me and kiss me on the steps of Widener Library. All these things he does with the Baywatch girl.

Am I being a voyeur? I am watching their private moments. Is my gaze intrusive? Is a gaze unnoticed by its recipients an intrusive gaze? I must see what Lacan says about it, but I suppose it is. I am intruding on their privacy. I have cracked their privacy shell. But how private is Harvard Yard? They are hugging and kissing in a public place. It is dark, but it is still public. Students come and go. Professors come and go. I have a *right* to look in a public place. I must discover what the Baywatch girl has that I have not.

If it is a matter of breasts, I also have two. My two breasts lack silicon, but at least they are somewhat cantilevered. Two cantilevered breasts surely can compete with two siliconed breasts. My cantilevered breasts have been pulleyed up, but they are natural. They are made of pure breast tissue. They have lobes that can generate milk. They have ducts that lead to the nipples. They are genuine mammary glands. If James squeeezes them, they will not feel unnatural. They are pure organic tissue.

There is a moral principle involved here. I am as God made me. James is getting the *real me*. I have neither been siliconed nor liposuctioned. No one has taken a vacuum to my hips, thighs, or buttocks. I have not tampered with nature. I am pure cotton, not polyester.

Wait. They are getting into the subway. I follow still at a discreet distance. At Park Street station they emerge, and walk to West Street. WEST STREET! Does James live on West Street?

Where Margaret worked daily at *The Dial*? Where she held the "Conversations"? Where she told the Boston women about Goddesses?

They enter a small brownstone at No. 10. I wait a moment, and then, under cloak of darkness, approach the door. His name is on the bell. There. There it is. James Apthorp, Apt. 4C.

I cross the street and look up at the fourth floor just as the lights flick on. I see their shadows against the lighted window. I watch them embrace again, then sink out of sight, like shadow puppets. Are they on the bed? His bed? Is that why they no longer appear?

I touch my face and find it wet. I did not realize I was crying. My M & M's cannot compete. My natural breasts cannot compete. I walk on slowly to my own apartment on Dartmouth Street. I wonder, suddenly, if Natasha Owens is still playing the tracking game and turn to look just before entering the house. I catch a flash of her white sneakers about a block behind me. I feel supported by her continued presence, by her refusal to give up on our "whole relationship." The next morning I find a letter in my box.

Dearest Angelica:

Why are you so afraid of love? Margaret wasn't. You know that. You have told me about Anna Barker and Cary. She let *them* into her heart. It was hard for her to accommodate both head and heart in a relationship in the nineteenth century. But women can do it now. With other women. So why do we need men? What do they do for us? What does James Apthorp *do* for you? I KNOW ALL ABOUT THE TWO OF YOU. I've watched you in Houghton . . . and after Houghton. I've followed you both home to your apartment. I've watched for him to leave. He leaves after he's USED YOU FOR HIS MALE PURPOSES. To accommodate his pole. His stick. To spill it out into you. You are just a UTENSIL for him to EMPTY INTO, to relieve himself. Is that what you want in a relationship? In love? To be a utensil?

I can offer you so much more. We are the same. We are WOMEN together. We don't have to submit to those repressive, patriarchal assholes. We don't need them. We can be Amazons. Goddesses. Now that we can procreate without them, we can exist without them. No betrayals. No infidelities. No competition. NO DENIAL OF MIND. With me you can be WHOLE. Not just a HOLE. Think about it

I love you.
Natasha

Oh God. Oh God. What do I do about this mad letter?

25

I have reached the black folder.

She has decided to return home. They will perhaps survive better at this moment in their lives in the States, where she can earn a living writing, and where her book on the Roman Republic has a better chance of publication than in Italy, where they are still political outcasts from her beloved Rome. Her friends at home are doubtful of her reception because of the child and the marriage/non-marriage.

After her death, Emerson writes:

It is a bitter satire on our social order . . . Margaret Fuller, having attained the highest & broadest culture that any American woman has possessed, came home with an Italian gentleman whom she had married, & their infant son, & perished by shipwreck on the rocks of Fire Island, off New York; and her friends said, "Well, on the whole, it was not so lamentable, & perhaps it was the best thing that could happen to her. For, had she lived, what could she have done? How could she have supported herself, her husband, & child?" And most persons, hearing this, acquiesced in this view that, after the education has gone far, such is the expensiveness of America, that the best use to put a fine woman to, is to drown her to save her board.

But I am getting ahead of my story. She is still alive. She has joined the expatriate community in Florence, having appeared to their surprise with her husband and child. Elizabeth Barrett Browning declares: "Nobody had even suspected a word of this underplot. The husband is a Roman marquis . . . with no pretension to cope with his wife on any ground appertaining to the intellect. She talks, & he listens. . . . "

Her marriage or non-marriage is a cause for much speculation. But little Nino plays with Browning's son Pen, six months younger, and the two women, who have not always admired each other, become friends.

She also renews a friendship with Joseph Mozier, a sculptor who now employs Ossoli in his studio while Margaret tutors his daughter. It is Mozier who after her death says damaging things to Hawthorne about Ossoli, whom he finds handsome, but "half an idiot," and who claims that Margaret's history of the Roman Republic never existed, contributing to Hawthorne's determination that she was "a humbug."

But much worse, in retrospect, is Mozier's role in helping Margaret to secure passage on the ill-fated ELIZABETH, a merchant freighter docked in Livorno that will be much cheaper than the Cunard liner from Liverpool. The freighter's cargo contains 150 tons of Carrara marble and Powers's statue of John Calhoun.

Margaret tells Elizabeth Browning that, though she is afraid of shipwreck, she takes the ship's name as a lucky sign. Her fears of shipwreck and drowning go far back to her earliest childhood. In an autobiographical romance written when she was 30, she wrote that, as a child, she had picked up a book Ellen Kilshaw had been reading, and read in Scott's *Guy Mannering* a description of the rocks on the seacoast where little Harry Bertram was lost:

> I was the little Harry Bartram and had lost her—all I had to lose—and sought her vainly in long dark caves that had no end, plashing through the water, while the crags beetled above, threatening to fall and crush the poor child. . . . [Ellen reentered the room and] I laid my head against her shoulder and wept—dimly feeling that I must lose her and all—all who spoke to me of the same things—that the cold wave must rush over me.

That fear of the cold wave stays with her throughout her life. Caroline Sturgis tells of Margaret's fear of the waves when they vacationed together at Cohasset. Margaret records in her journal for 1842, that while sleeping with Anna on Sam's pillow:

> I had a frightful dream of being imprisoned in a ship at sea, the waves all dashing round, and knowing that the crew had resolved to throw me in. While in horrible suspense,

many persons that I knew came on board. At first they seemed delighted to see me & wished to talk but when I let them know my danger...intimated a hope that they might save me, with cold courtliness glided away. Oh it was horrible these averted faces and well dressed figures turning from me, from captive, with the cold wave rushing up into which I was to be thrown.

Five years later, when she suspected her pregnancy, she wrote to Emerson: "I am tired of keeping myself up in the water without corks, and without strength to swim." Once assured of her pregnancy, she had written, we remember, to a friend, using a plunging ship as metaphor: "...the drama of my fate is very deep, and the ship plunges deeper as it rises higher."

Now she boards the doomed ELIZABETH early in May 1850, writing the Storys to "look out for news of shipwreck," with her "head full of boxes, bundles, pots of jelly & phials of medicine" and a goat for Nino's milk, and on May 17th, finally sets sail with her husband and child, having been delayed by the loading of marble, the fateful 150 tons of marble.

The Captain, Captain Hasty, soon contracts smallpox and dies early in June as they reach Gibraltar. They are quarantined for a week and start out again, but soon little Nino contracts the disease, despite the vaccinations Margaret had worked hard to secure for him. The Ossolis fight for his life and nurse him so lovingly they bring him back to health.

After the death of the captain, the second mate, Henry Bangs, is in charge. After more than a month at sea, they are swept off course by strong winds. Bangs thinks they are near Cape May, New Jersey, but actually they are near another popular summer resort, Point of Woods, on Fire Island. A tropical hurricane has been disrupting shipping along the Atlantic coast. The storm hits the ELIZABETH in the middle of the night. The ship hits a sandbar, and the water Margaret has always feared pours through the hole. The ship has indeed been Hastyed and Banged.

Margaret gives her life preserver to a sailor who will go for help. Mrs. Hasty makes it to shore lashed to a plank with the second mate behind her. Captain Bangs survives as well, though washed ashore "insensible." Most of the crew abandon ship. Margaret won't leave her baby. Five of the crew remain with the Ossoli party. The storm has riled the sea up. The waves are terrifying. But there are people on shore, perhaps just a few hundred yards away. Perhaps even less. Their presence offers hope that they will be rescued.

There are at least three accounts of how Margaret died:

1. She drowned in the forecastle, while her husband, son, maid Celeste and the five crew members remained there with her. (Husband, son, maid, and three of the crew to die later.)
2. She died, about to step onto a plank, believing her son and husband already launched, and a wave washed her away.
3. She remained on the forecastle until the last with her husband, when Bates, the Steward, took her child and

tried to make it to shore on a plank. The steward's and
child's bodies washed up later.
An American friend, Horace Sumner, also on board with the
Ossolis, was, like them, never found.

There are at least 2 accounts of why they weren't rescued:
1. The storm prevented a lifeboat from reaching them.
2. The scavengers, who were waiting on shore, didn't
    choose to save them, because they didn't know anyone
    important was on board.

So the circumstances of her death are like her marriage/non-
marriage. Ambiguous. Mysterious. The stuff of rumor and
speculation.

She is gone. Thoreau retrieves the button from Ossoli's coat.
Her manuscript on the history of the Roman Republic is
never found. But the Margaret-Ghost remains.

26

I have brought my own manuscript to completion and am preparing it for submission to the department. I am distracted by both James and Natasha Owens, who continues to follow me and send me notes about the patriarchy.

James has become even more sullen and uncommunicative. He no longer comes to my bed. He grudgingly continues our M & M conversations on breaks at Houghton.

ANGELICA: My book on Margaret is finished.

JAMES: God! Melville is still nowhere near finished. My committee is losing patience with me, but I've been so hooked on Melville's depressions I still haven't dealt with his intimate knowledge of whales.

ANGELICA: The Japanese are eating even more whales now. The whole rest of the world is alarmed that they're not protecting the species.

JAMES: Melville thought the whale was eternal. Nothing is eternal.

ANGELICA: Love is eternal, James.

JAMES: Fuck love. What kind of nonsense is that? You sound like your batty Margaret. Give it up, Angelica. She was just a frustrated old maid.

ANGELICA: She wasn't! She married and had a child.

JAMES: You told me yourself what Mozier said! Ossoli was a half-idiot.

ANGELICA: Hardly that. She had just given up on literary friendships—on intellectual friendships.

JAMES: Are *you* giving up on intellectual friendships?

ANGELICA: I don't want to, James. Should I? Should I give up on our intellectual friendship?

I want to ask if this is all we have, all we have ever had, but I fear his answer. He grunts at me. I don't know if he is saying yes or no. I change the subject.

ANGELICA: Melville must be turning in his grave. No more whales? I can't believe in their extinction.

JAMES: They won't stop killing them. The economics of it is too tempting.

ANGELICA: Have you ever eaten whale meat?

JAMES: Have *you?*

Our conversations have come to this. They are no longer even intellectual conversations. They are strained. Distant. Impersonal. I wish I could ask him if there is any hope for us now that the Baywatch girl is there. I don't. Again, I'm afraid of his answer.

I leave him to go home alone and think about us, about how I can compete with her, how I can seduce him back to my bed, how I can regain his love—if, indeed, I ever had it. I know that for now it is gone, but perhaps she is just a pair of siliconed breasts. We could mean so much to each other. I could mean so much to him. I could help him in his work. We have interests to share. And not only interests. Dreams. Why will he not understand that there is more to a relationship than siliconed breasts? Why is not a Victoria's Secret cantilever good enough?

Why doesn't my MIND gain me some points? Why can't our intellectual friendship continue and thrive, and develop for him into true love? Is what I feel for James true love? Or is it simply obsession? What do I want from him? What does he want from me? If I am no longer anything to him, why does he still sit beside me in Houghton? I must mean *something* to him. I must *matter*.

The Baywatch girl is just a phase. All men like huge breasts. All men are threatened by women of intellect. Margaret's experience should teach me that.

But this is now and that was then. Now and then are worlds apart in time/space, education, knowledge, mores, male/female relationships. Now we know that Men are from Mars and Women are from Venus, and if they can bridge the psychological distance between the two planets, if they can engage in proper interplanetary travel and colonization, they can have it all. They don't need NASA. Everyone can go to

Barnes and Noble and figure it out for themselves. They can read the book in the coffee shop. They don't even have to buy it. They can read the feminist literature and the books in the Gay/Lesbian section. They can see how in a Jungian sense everything floods into everything else.

They don't even have to go to Houghton or Harvard to do it. They can also learn from daytime TV, where mothers talk about sleeping with their daughters' husbands and fathers talk about sleeping with their daughters, and guys with guys and girls with girls. It is all very democratic.

Now is very different than then. I have it better than Margaret, don't I? Isn't everything open to me?

27

The next time James leaves with the Baywatch girl, I follow them again. This time they do not sink out of sight. This time their shadows move differently against the lighted window. I cannot bear it. I cannot bear what I know they are doing. What I see them doing.

I ring the downstairs bell. No answer. I ring another bell. Someone buzzes me up. I walk up to the fourth floor, holding on to the banister, because I don't feel quite steady. My hands are clammy. I feel crazed. I must stop what they are doing. I ring the bell for Apartment 4C. I keep ringing it, and the sound echoes through the hallway. It is very loud. I hope I have jarred them out of the Act. They were engaged, I know, in the Act. I must stop them. The bell continues to sound. My finger is stuck to it as James must be stuck to the Baywatch girl.

It is a long time before he comes. When he does, he is wearing a towel.

ANGELICA (*politely*): Good evening, James.

JAMES: What the HELL!

ANGELICA: May I come in? (*I enter as I speak.*)

JAMES: What?

ANGELICA: We must talk James.

JAMES: Now?

ANGELICA: I know she is here.

JAMES: It's none of your business who is here.

ANGELICA: But it *is* my business, James. I may not be siliconed, but I am better for you.

The Baywatch girl emerges, wearing a man's robe, James's robe. Her long blonde hair cascades around her like loops of semen. I can see her in a lithograph by Munch. She is archetypical.

BAYWATCH GIRL: Who is it James?

JAMES: No one . . . no one at all.

ANGELICA: But I *am* someone James. We have a special friendship. We can talk about Margaret and Melville. (*pointing to the Baywatch girl*) Does she even know who Queequeg is? (*To the Baywatch girl:*) Do you know who Queequeg is? We can discuss literature and ideas, James. I can help you to fulfill your intellectual potential. I can enrich you, more than you can imagine. We can GROW TOGETHER!

JAMES: Angelica. Go home before you embarrass yourself even more.

ANGELICA: But I am so good for you, James. I can offer you so much more than she can.

(*The Baywatch girl is watching me silently with smug eyes.*)

BAYWATCH GIRL: Are you coming back to bed, James?

JAMES: YES! Yes.

He looks at me with pain, distress, or embarrassment (I am not sure which) in his blue eyes. Blue like James Nathan's eyes. Blue.

He follows her into the back room and closes the door.

He leaves me standing there. I am standing in the middle of his apartment, offering him M & M's he no longer wants. The chocolate has gone stale. It is covered with a white, ghost-like bloom. It is now inedible.

When I leave the apartment, I see Natasha Owens, as always, flashing her white sneakers a block away. This time, instead of ignoring her, I strike out in her direction. I expect her to retreat but she does not. She knows what I have seen. She did not have to see it herself to know. She waits until I approach and reaches out to embrace me. I shove her arm away. She is startled.

ANGELICA: Go away!

NATASHA: He doesn't deserve you. No man does.

ANGELICA: Go away, Natasha. I don't want you either. I don't want anyone. Just leave me alone.

Even in the dim streetlight, I can see her pale. I have rejected her. I have rejected her "whole relationship." I regret it. I know how I have suffered from James's rejection. I know how Margaret suffered. But I cannot help it. Right now I do not want any relationship. I just want to go home.

28

The committee has my manuscript. They have been reading it for the past two weeks. I will hear from them shortly. I have spent these past two weeks alone, free of my manuscript, just thinking of Margaret. She was a phenomenon. A force, as Sam Ward said. When George Eliot read the *Memoirs*, which were published two years after her death—even in the state they were in, her papers corrupted and edited by Emerson, Clarke, and Channing—she was most touched by the passage she remembered from Margaret's journal: "I shall always reign through the intellect, but the life! the life! O my God shall that never be sweet?"

How sweet was it, finally, in Italy, under the umbrella pines in that gentler, flowing landscape so beloved by American expatriate artists and writers from her century into our own? We all know the sacrifices that "life" makes for intellect, but none more than the woman of intellect whose mind makes men uncomfortable.

How was it for Margaret when Ossoli, understanding nothing of intellect, approached her as a woman only, a woman he could love and desire? How was it when for the first time, intellect was not a barrier to the sweetness of life, to full womanly being and the motherhood she so deeply desired, to Jung's Eros above all? Yet even before this, it was her womanliness that had leavened her intellect with passion and compassion, her womanliness that enabled her to write so eloquently of the mad and the sad (prostitutes, criminals, the marginalized). It was her full womanliness that led her to want love, to seek it everywhere, in men and women, to offer love and demand its return. LOVE ME! she said. YOU MUST LOVE ME!

As Natasha said to me.
As I said to James.
As Margaret said to *her* James.

I have received a call from John Denton, who has not yet been displaced by Natasha's researches. The committee has read my book and would like to meet with me in the department office this afternoon.

I walk across the green to the college. I take an extra few minutes to visit the site of Margaret's former *Dial* offices on West Street. I think about the transformations of almost 150 years. What would she make of the Greek wine bar that stands where she offered the "Conversations" to the ladies of

Boston? Is it not fitting, since she tried so hard to inform them about Goddesses? Greek Goddesses? To stoke up their pride in their womanly intellects? To make them proud of their erudition? To encourage them to reach for the exquisite merger of intellect and womanliness, to reach for the sweetness of life while retaining intellect? To encourage them to be whole?

On my way back, I pass James's apartment. *Das ist hart*, as Margaret said to James Nathan. *Das ist hart*. What will happen to James's manuscript? To his tenure? I have not seen him since I submitted my manuscript. Is he still immersed in Melville's depression? Has he at least proceeded to the whales? Has the Baywatch girl distracted him even more, now that I no longer visit Houghton? Now that our M & M's have gone stale? But I must not think of James now. Only of my own manuscript. Only of the committee and their decision.

The door to the department office is closed. John Denton wants privacy today. It is an omen, but whether for good or bad I am not sure. I knock and he responds. When I enter, he is surrounded by the entire department: Bill Lipton, who today seems fleshier than ever, the Jordaens Bacchus sitting (uncharacteristically) in judgment; Margaretta Sinclair, looking pale and worried, her graying hair a disturbed birds' nest; Natasha Owens, with a look in her eye that I cannot quite read. Regret? Sympathy? Malice?

John Denton looks at me and does not look at me, but at some point on the floor in front of him. His bow tie is crooked. His pipe is unlit in his mouth. The room is very still. It is filled with tension. I think of the ectoplasm that fills rooms in seances. Ectoplasm is blue-gray and filmy, transparent. It floats. This stuff—this tension—is heavy and dark. It seems black, but I cannot be sure of the color, only of its weight. If it is as heavy as it feels, it could squash me out of pure gravity. It is an *Inquisition*. I can feel it. Like Spain in the 1490s, when they expelled the Jews. Like the Council of Trent in sixteenth-century Italy. It does not feel like Boston at the end of the twentieth century. It does not even feel like Margaret's Boston.

JOHN DENTON: Professor Bookbinder, your teaching record seems fine. The students enjoy your classes. And you've been a good college citizen. You've served on several committees.

Ah yes, I think to myself. I've served on all those God-awful committees, where people talk for the sake of hearing themselves talk, or for the petty power of it. Is this what I am dealing with now? This COMMITTEE? What about my book? What about Margaret?

I find out soon enough.

John Denton raises his eyes and looks at me. He looks around him at his colleagues. They communicate soundlessly, through their gazes. Margaretta Sinclair looks first at him, then, sympathetically, at me. From Natasha Owens and Bill Lipton I sense no compassion.

JOHN DENTON: Professor Bookbinder. Under normal circumstances, we would tell you of our decision by mail. But (*he looks around him for reassurance*) since we are in

agreement, I see no reason to prolong what must be your
apprehension.

He does not have to say it. I know. But he is the speaker,
the one in charge. The one who must deliver the judgment
of the group. He must announce their opinion of my work.
He must offer up their decision about my fate, a decision that
will affect the rest of my life. He must, in fact, articulate the
reason for their vote.

And so it goes. The department feels unanimously that
I have spoken too much of love and not enough of intellect.
I have not examined Margaret's radical social theories. I
have not determined whether or not she actually read
Marx, though she knew of him. (She did read Fourier, but I
did not even deal with that.) I have not dealt with her literary criticism or with her extraordinary war dispatches from
Italy, or her translations of Goethe, or her interest in both
mesmerism and mysticism, or the detailed subjects of her
enlightened "Conversations" or her writings in *The Dial*, or
the influence of her pioneering feminism (a subject Natasha
Owens especially found wanting). In short, it is for her
intellectual contribution to American culture that Margaret
is so justly famed, and I have not dealt sufficiently with that.

John Denton looks embarrassed as he finishes his litany
of "have-nots." There is no point in telling him that I did deal
with some of these things, but that love was what mattered
most to her. That she wanted fully to use her woman's heart.
He would not understand. As to Natasha Owens and Bill
Lipton, from whom I might have expected some under-

standing, it is clear that even with them, my understanding of love and theirs is quite different. I have not been political, about either sex or love. But then, neither was Margaret.

John Denton looks down once more at the floor. He fusses at his crooked tie.

JOHN DENTON: Professor Bookbinder, though we've enjoyed having you with us and are grateful for all your efforts on behalf of the students and the college, we regret very much that under the circumstances, we are unable to grant you a tenured position in this department.

I have lost everything.

I have lost James to someone who doesn't even know who Queequeg is.

I have lost the lifelong security of tenure, because the department doesn't understand love.

I should feel totally rejected, but I feel instead strangely liberated. When you have lost everything, there is nothing left but possibility.

They have given me my freedom—all of them. Like Margaret, I have tired of intellectual friendships. As she wrote in *Woman in the Nineteenth Century*, "Woman is born for love and it is impossible to turn her from seeking it."

I am free now to go to Italy. It was wise of me to make my reservations last week.

I leave tomorrow for Rome.

ANGELICA BOOKBINDER'S SELECTED READING LIST

Chevigny, Bell Gale. *The Woman and the Myth: Margaret Fuller's Life & Writings,* Boston: Northeastern University Press, Revised and expanded, 1994. (Originally published 1976.)

Deiss, Joseph Jay. *The Roman Years of Margaret Fuller,* New York: T.Y. Crowell, 1969.

Emerson, Ralph Waldo. *Emerson in His Journals,* Edited by Joel Porte. Cambridge: Harvard University Press, 1982.

Emerson, Ralph Waldo. *The Journals and Miscellaneous Notebooks of Ralph Waldo Emerson,* Edited by William H. Gilman et al., Cambridge: Harvard University Press, 1960.

Emerson, R.W.; Channing, W.H.; Clarke, J.F. *Memoirs of Margaret Fuller Ossoli,* 2 vols. Boston: Phillips, Sampson and Company, 1852.

Fuller, Margaret. "The Great Lawsuit: Man vs. Men, Woman vs. Women," *The Dial,* IV, no. 1 (July 1843)

Fuller, Margaret. *The Letters of Margaret Fuller,* Edited by Robert N. Hudspeth, 6 vols., Ithaca: Cornell University Press, 1983–1994.

Fuller, Margaret. *Essays on American Life and Letters,* Edited by Joel Myerson, New Haven: Yale University Press, 1978.

Fuller, Margaret. *Woman in the Nineteenth Century,* New York: Greeley & McElrath, 1845. Reprint. New York: W.W. Norton. 1971.

Fuller, Margaret. *Margaret Fuller's New York Journalism,* Edited by Catherine C. Mitchell, Knoxville: University of Tennessee Press, 1995.

Herbert, T. Walter. *Dearest Beloved: The Hawthornes and the Making of the Middle Class Family,* Berkeley: University of California Press, 1993.

Hofstadter, Dan. *The Love Affair As a Work of Art,* New York: Farrar, Strauss and Giroux, 1996.

Love-Letters of Margaret Fuller, 1845-1846, Introduction by Julia Ward Howe. New York: 1903. Reprint. New York: AMS Press, 1970.

McAleer, John. *Ralph Waldo Emerson: Days of Encounter,* Boston: Little, Brown & Co., 1984.

Miller, Edward Haviland. *Herman Melville,* New York: George Braziller, Inc., 1975.

Von Mehren, Joan. *Minerva and the Muse: A Life of Margaret Fuller,* Amherst: University of Massachusetts Press, 1994.